THE LYON AND THE BLUESTOCKING

The Lyon's Den Connected World

E.L. Johnson

DRAGONBLADE PUBLISHING, INC.

ARE YOU SIGNED UP FOR DRAGONBLADE'S BLOG?

You'll get the latest news and information on exclusive giveaways, exclusive excerpts, coming releases, sales, free books, cover reveals and more.

Check out our complete list of authors, too!

No spam, no junk. That's a promise!

Sign Up Here

www.dragonbladepublishing.com

Dearest Reader;

Thank you for your support of a small press. At Dragonblade Publishing, we strive to bring you the highest quality Historical Romance from some of the best authors in the business. Without your support, there is no 'us', so we sincerely hope you adore these stories and find some new favorite authors along the way.

Happy Reading!

CEO, Dragonblade Publishing

Additional Dragonblade books by Author E.L. Johnson

The Perfect Poison Murders

The Strangled Servant (Book 1)

The Poisoned Clergyman (Book 2)

The Mistress Murders (Book 3)

The Deadly Debutante (Book 4)

The Lyon's Den Series

The Lyon and the Bluestocking

Other Lyon's Den Books

Into the Lyon's Den by Jade Lee

The Scandalous Lyon by Maggi Andersen

Fed to the Lyon by Mary Lancaster

The Lyon's Lady Love by Alexa Aston

The Lyon's Laird by Hildie McQueen

The Lyon Sleeps Tonight by Elizabeth Ellen Carter

A Lyon in Her Bed by Amanda Mariel

Fall of the Lyon by Chasity Bowlin

Lyon's Prey by Anna St. Claire

Loved by the Lyon by Collette Cameron

The Lyon's Den in Winter by Whitney Blake

Kiss of the Lyon by Meara Platt

Always the Lyon Tamer by Emily E K Murdoch

To Tame the Lyon by Sky Purington

How to Steal a Lyon's Fortune by Alanna Lucas

The Lyon's Surprise by Meara Platt

A Lyon's Pride by Emily Royal

Lyon Eyes by Lynne Connolly

Tamed by the Lyon by Chasity Bowlin

Lyon Hearted by Jade Lee

The Devilish Lyon by Charlotte Wren

Lyon in the Rough by Meara Platt

Lady Luck and the Lyon by Chasity Bowlin

Rescued by the Lyon by C.H. Admirand

Pretty Little Lyon by Katherine Bone

The Courage of a Lyon by Linda Rae Sande

Pride of Lyons by Jenna Jaxon

The Lyon's Share by Cerise DeLand

The Heart of a Lyon by Anna St. Claire

Into the Lyon of Fire by Abigail Bridges
Lyon of the Highlands by Emily Royal
The Lyon's Puzzle by Sandra Sookoo
Lyon at the Altar by Lily Harlem
Captivated by the Lyon by C.H. Admirand
The Lyon's Secret by Laura Trentham
The Talons of a Lyon by Jude Knight
The Lyon and the Lamb by Elizabeth Keysian
To Claim a Lyon's Heart by Sherry Ewing
A Lyon of Her Own by Anna St. Claire
Don't Wake a Sleeping Lyon by Sara Adrien

CHAPTER ONE

17 Marlborough Place, London
February 1814

E LIZABETH DENHAM WINCED as her mother's shrill voice filled the small dining room.

"This is too vulgar to be discussed. I cannot abide history discussions at the breakfast table, Elizabeth, I simply cannot," Mrs. Denham, of the Devonshire Denhams, said.

Elizabeth looked up from her teacup and felt the full force of her mother's glare. "But Mama, the Mongols, it's such a fascinating history…" She faltered.

Her mother, a stern woman with a plump face and wispy hair that threatened to escape from her stiff mob cap, frowned. "No. I will have none of that at the table. Why can't you be more like your sister?"

Elizabeth glanced at her younger sibling, a young woman with soft blond curls and a rosy complexion, who sat admiring her reflection in a spoon. "Annabelle."

"What, Lizzie?" Annabelle's eyes never left the spoon as she patted down a stray blonde hair.

"Never mind," Elizabeth muttered into her tea. "But Mama, don't you want to know about the history of the Mongols? I've just been reading about them. Genghis Khan, their leader, was truly fearsome. But if you don't like that, have you read the paper this morning? A volcano has erupted in the Philippines, a real live volcano. Isn't that terrifying?"

"No Mongols, no Genghis Khans, and no volcanoes. Not at the breakfast table." Mrs. Denham set down her bone china teacup with a sharp clatter. "Last week it was the Crusades. I've had quite enough, young lady. We will only have civilized talk here, and no mention of Mongols. I trust you will make more appropriate conversation this afternoon when we take tea at the Plimpetts'."

"The Plimpetts'?" Elizabeth felt a shiver of dread come over her.

"Tea?" Annabelle looked up.

"Trust you would pull your attention away for that." Elizabeth smirked.

Annabelle stuck her tongue out at her older sister. "So? If there's tea that means company, and good company means fashion and good discussion. What shall we wear today to go out?" Annabelle rested her elbows on the table and put her chin in her hand, eyeing her sister's humble clothes and fair, angular face. "Something blue perhaps, to bring out your eyes."

Elizabeth had startling gray eyes, or so she'd been told. Like the stormy gray of choppy seas before an oncoming storm. She liked it, as if there were hidden depths to uncover.

"Never mind the clothes, Annabelle, you always look charming. Now Elizabeth, remember. What have I told you about talking before? No one wants to hear about your history lessons, girl. If you cannot talk about anything sensible, keep your remarks to the weather," her mother said. "At least Mrs. Plimpett will provide civil conversation, which is more than I can say for you."

Elizabeth frowned, practically a mirror reflection of her mother's displeased expression. They might be related, but she felt she had little in common with her mother, aside from a long neck, light skin that tanned to a burnished gold in the sun, and long silken dark hair.

The Plimpetts were a family of longstanding friendship to the Denhams (so they said) and longstanding suffering (so they endeavored to convince others) due to their being unable to find any young man to meet their exacting standards, as befitting the beauty of their daughters, Philippa and Harriet.

Mrs. Denham and Mrs. Plimpett had become friends years ago, when they had been debutantes at the same London Season, and had maintained a polite relationship ever since. With each older woman having daughters, it was naturally assumed that the close friendship would continue.

Unfortunately, when it came to Elizabeth, her taciturn nature and tendency to be distracted by books did not serve her well when it came time to be sociable. As a result, she rather dreaded seeing the Plimpett girls, particularly the eldest, Philippa.

After years of trying to follow her mother's wish and be polite and friendly toward the Denham sisters, Philippa now viewed Elizabeth with a sort of thinly veiled disregard, poorly hidden behind open amusement at whatever sensible thing Elizabeth said.

In Elizabeth's mind, it didn't matter what she wore. Philippa would find a way to make her the butt of a joke regardless, and Philippa's younger sister Harriet would be confused at the conversation, for she read little else besides ladies' fashion periodicals.

After a brief discussion with her sister, Elizabeth wore a plain, cobalt blue dress, long sleeves, no frills, but with a white gauzy underlay material beneath for warmth. As she looked over the pages of the history book in her lap, she didn't take in a single word. The forthcoming tea party filled every ounce of her being with dread.

At the respectable hour, Elizabeth joined Annabelle and her mother in the foyer of their London townhouse. They were not members of the ton, nor had they any superior rank or title. But the men in their family had kept a very good sort of glove shop, and made smart business decisions, which had allowed the glove shop to prosper.

What had begun as an ordinary shop in Essex had grown into a handful, including a respectable one in London itself, off of Bond Street. As a result, the family had been a family of means for years, and whilst they had no qualms about their humble origins or current success, their stoic awareness of their situation meant they took each day as it came, with the knowledge that at any moment, their fortunes could prosper more or fail entirely. Such was the life of a tradesman, and his family.

Elizabeth knew as well as her mother that despite their wealth, she and her sister had little chance of entering the ranks of the aristocracy unless by marriage, or if the men in their family provided some service to the king. And with Elizabeth as the oldest and expected to marry first, she saw that hope die in her mother's eyes at her every mention of historical facts.

Elizabeth swallowed as she donned her hooded, pale sea-green cloak and tied the strings at her throat. She pulled on a pair of expertly made soft kid gloves her father had fashioned just for her and looked upon her reflection in the small looking glass that hung in the foyer.

She joined her mother and sister in a comfortable carriage and in a matter of minutes, they entered a respectable neighborhood in Cheapside, where Mrs. Plimpett, a round woman whose family was also in trade (yet not as prosperous), lived.

Upon their entry into the simple white drawing room, which boasted floor-length curtains the color of champagne, as well as a matching sofa and similarly upholstered wooden chairs, the girls were bid to sit down amidst the company of Mrs. Plimpett's daughters and two young men, a Mr. Hickson and Mr. Cox.

Mr. Hickson had short-cropped blond hair with a touch of silver at the hairline, an angular face, and a cleft in his chin. He greeted the girls with a politeness that did not reach his eyes and observed the Denham girls' beauty a bit longer than was necessary.

Mr. Cox was a short, round man with thinning, blond hair that clustered around his temple and ears. He needed a haircut but had tried to comb his hair in a way that almost seemed fashionable, but wasn't. He wore a dark suit jacket and cream waistcoat with buttons that strained over his stomach. His neck was swathed in layers of fussily tied white cravat that gave him the overall appearance of being stuffed into a suit, ready to explode at any moment. He gave the Denham girls a once-over look and then returned his attention to the pastries and tarts upon the long oval table that stood at the center of the chairs.

After introductions had been made, the two matrons left to chat in Mrs. Plimpett's parlor, leaving the younger members of the group to socialize over tea. Elizabeth wondered if something was amiss, for Philippa kept shooting little expectant looks at Mr. Hickson as if she expected him to propose any minute.

Elizabeth quietly sipped her tea and tried to remain calm as the others spoke of the weather. Just when she thought she might die of boredom, Mr. Hickson said, "It's a shame about this volcano exploding, isn't it?"

The other women looked confused as Elizabeth leaned forward with interest. Finally, a man of some sense. She answered, "Yes, terrible news. I read that over a thousand people died."

"Who?" Philippa asked.

"People in the Philippines. It's been all over the papers, Mount Mayon exploded," Elizabeth said.

"Yes, that's right," Mr. Hickson said, his eyes looking over her curves before meeting her eyes. "It's nice to meet a young lady who keeps aware of current events."

Elizabeth brightened as Philippa's expression darkened and she said with a sly smile, "Dear Miss Denham isn't just knowledgeable about current events, she knows all about history too, don't you, Miss Denham?"

"Yes, I like history. This volcano, from what I've read, it is terrible but not so devastating as that of Pompeii."

"Pomp what?" Philippa asked.

"Pompeii," Elizabeth repeated. "A city in Italy. When Mount Vesuvius exploded, it allegedly destroyed towns and cities for miles around."

Mr. Hickson said, "That was the fifth century, wasn't it?"

"The first century, I believe," Elizabeth said.

"Oh. My mistake." He reddened and looked away.

His companion, Mr. Cox, looked at her as if she were an interesting sort of insect. "You know history, do you?"

"Yes, I like to make a study of it. There's so much to learn."

Mr. Cox scratched his round chin, where a short stubble grew. "You're an educated sort of female, I suppose. That's singular. I thought most girls read the ladies' journal and studied fashion plates."

"I imagine they do," Elizabeth said. "But I was just reading about Genghis Khan and the Mongol hordes this morning—"

"How charming, that you know so much useful information, Miss Denham." Philippa cut her off, giggled, and exchanged a coy smile with her sister, before saying, "She knows so much of history. I do declare, Miss Denham, sometimes I wonder if you're just making it all up, your stories are so fantastical."

"They are not fantastical, it's real history—" Elizabeth started when Annabelle stepped on her foot.

Elizabeth glanced at her, receiving a warning look. Elizabeth looked from her sister to their hosts, then at the young gentlemen who smiled at the girls. She'd done it again. Opened her mouth and ruined all hope of making polite conversation. Judging from Philippa's triumphant smile, she'd gone and put her foot in it for sure.

Mr. Cox swallowed a mouthful of blackberry tart, wiped his

mouth, shedding crumbs everywhere, and said, "What pretty dresses you girls are wearing. I say, is that silk? Wherever did you buy that?"

Elizabeth turned pink, sat back against the sofa in quiet despair, and sipped her tea. She offered no more comment and left the conversation to the others. Annabelle rallied and kept the conversation going by complimenting the Plimpett girls on their dresses and asking whether they had toured the parks recently.

Once the girls' visit had ended and Mrs. Plimpett bid them a good day, Elizabeth was the first out of the house, darting down the steps to the sidewalk. The moment she was safely inside the family carriage, she slumped against the comfortable seats in relief.

"Well, how did that go, girls? Did you enjoy yourselves?" Their mother asked, climbing in beside her. Seeing their pinched expressions, she asked, "Oh no. What happened?"

Annabelle shot Elizabeth a glance and said, "It was fine. The Plimpett girls are such founts of conversation, we always come away more informed than before. Such good conversation and pretty dresses."

Mrs. Denham knew better. She arched a delicate brown eyebrow and pulled out a fan, gracefully wafting the air from herself. "Elizabeth?"

Elizabeth sighed. "I made a hash of it, Mama." She relayed her social gaffe.

"Oh, Lizzie," her mother said. "You see? This is what happens when you talk too much about history. No one cares about your Mongols or volcanoes."

"It's not her fault, Mama. Those men weren't particularly well educated themselves. They'd much rather have talked about the latest fashions," Annabelle pointed out.

"Even so. It behooves you to take an interest in the general conversation, rather than go off on tangents on history. Really, Lizzie. This is why you're not invited out anywhere," Mrs. Denham said, shutting her fan with a loud snap.

"Is that really the sort of company you wish me to keep, Mama? The girls barely read the papers, and didn't know anything about the volcano that erupted a few weeks ago."

"Never mind the other girls, it's you both I care about." Mrs. Denham gave a little noise of exasperation and sat back as the carriage took them through the bustling streets of London. "Mrs. Plimpett tells me that the elder Miss Plimpett is to be engaged imminently to a young man of fortune. A Mr. Hickson, of five thousand a year." She looked at Elizabeth.

Elizabeth felt positively queasy, and it was not due to the rocking of the carriage against the bumpy London roads. This old argument again. Ever since she had turned sixteen, her mother had dragged her, and eventually her younger sister, to tea parties and along with her to pay social calls to matrons with eligible young men around town. Not that it did much but make Elizabeth feel awkward in the company of others.

Annabelle glanced at Elizabeth quickly. "How fortunate for Miss Plimpett."

"It is a good match, to be sure. But I had so wished that you would be engaged too by now, Lizzie. I was married at sixteen, and it was the best thing I could have done. There is so much pleasure to be had in owning your own home." Seeing Elizabeth's face, Mrs. Denham added, "But not if you talk the ears off of a man with constant chatter or bore him to tears with all this talk about history and the Mongols. For god's sake, Lizzie, leave it alone. Why can't you read something decent for once, like the *Lady's Magazine*?"

"But Mama—"

"Enough. I despair of you finding a husband, honestly. At least you have money, so you don't need to worry about marrying for an income. You can thank your father for that." Mrs. Denham patted Annabelle's knee. "You girls can afford to marry for love. But still, it wouldn't hurt to try and make normal conversation with people. You might get invited to parties for once, instead of always going to libraries and that dull bookseller's shop."

"Mama, enough. I understand." Elizabeth looked away.

"I don't think you do. It is high time for you to think about marriage, Lizzie. Your father and I can only look after you for so long before… well. Let's just say that Mrs. Plimpett was very proud of her daughter's accomplishments in matrimony, and she didn't even ask about you. Can you imagine why this would be?"

"I don't know," Elizabeth mumbled.

"Because she knows you have no prospects, and it hurts me to have to see her look so self-satisfied. I had thought that with your good sense and beauty, it wouldn't matter to gentlemen if you were a bluestocking."

"Mama…" Elizabeth uttered.

"It is true, and you had best get used to the word, especially if you keep patronizing libraries and bookshops. No, Lizzie, I now worry that you won't find anyone to marry." Her mother blinked hard and looked out at the view.

"Perhaps you are looking in the wrong place, Mama. If the gentlemen are so dull as those we met today, maybe a different sort of man would suit Lizzie," Annabelle said, a smile on her face. "A pirate, perhaps."

"Or a rake," Elizabeth said with a grin.

"A philistine."

"A Mongol."

"Girls, girls. Enough of that. This is serious," Mrs. Denham said, as the girls laughed.

Elizabeth was grateful for her sister's support, but her smile soon faded. Joke they might, but she had no marriage prospects, and it would simply be a matter of time before people began to talk or assume the worst.

No more was spoken of for the rest of the journey home. Once inside Elizabeth fled to her father's library, which was well stocked. She curled up on a comfortable faded blue-gray bench seat and glanced out the window at the dull buildings and smoking rooftops of the London houses.

At the advancing age of twenty-two, she had little wish to marry, particularly if the man was an obnoxious type like the boorish men she had encountered that afternoon. But she did wonder what it would be like, to not just share a household and a life, but to share a bed with a man.

Her cheeks blushed and she banished the thought quickly, as such rude thoughts were unbecoming and immodest. Her mother would surely disapprove. But neither could she stand to be a spinster all her life. Her mother's words rankled her and gave light to one of her own fears.

What if her mother was right, and no one really cared about history at all, but her? She set aside her book on the Mongols and instead went to one of the back rooms in the townhouse, which was used for storage. It was a small room with peeling wallpaper that smelled, and inside it was full of old coats, chairs that needed repair and reupholstering, and old toys from their childhood, as well as a small pianoforte.

Elizabeth was confident about few things, but her skills in music were one of them. She pulled out a set of much-used sheet music and let out an anguished sigh. She felt she could hardly exist without her books and piano. As her fingers touched the keys, she exhaled a loud sigh and began to relax at the sound of the first chords. She began to play, letting out her anger and aggression on the splatter of black and white keys, her fingers taking her worries away.

A pleasant hour passed where she played simpler country songs, and a new tune by Beethoven. Now relaxed, Elizabeth had thought the stresses of her day were over, until dinner the following evening, when over a glass of wine and dish of lamb chops, her mother said, "I wonder, Lizzie, whether you might like to join me for a bit of entertainment tonight."

"Of course, Mama. Were you thinking of a concert or a play?" Elizabeth asked, slicing into her chop.

"Oh yes, I'd love to see a new play," Annabelle said. "It's been ages since we've gone."

"I'm sorry Annabelle, but this is just for Elizabeth and me," Mrs. Denham said.

"Why?"

Mrs. Denham locked eyes across the table with her husband, who appeared half-asleep. "Just a chance for us to spend some time together, that's all."

"Where are we going, Mama? To an evening concert?" Elizabeth asked.

"Not quite. We're going to visit an acquaintance of mine, Mrs. Dove-Lyon." She smiled at Elizabeth, but her smile was not kind. It was businesslike, hard, even. It sent a shiver down Elizabeth's spine.

"But it's too late to pay a social call," Annabelle pointed out.

"Mrs. Dove-Lyon keeps late hours. She has invited us personally to attend her at a party this evening," Mrs. Denham said.

Elizabeth exchanged a look with her sister. Whatever her mother had planned, it was not good. Of that, she was certain.

Later that evening, the girls' maid, Peggy, knocked and entered Elizabeth's room. "Hello, Miss. I'm to help dress you for tonight."

Elizabeth had lain on her stomach on her bed and looked up from her book. "Dress me? What do you mean? I'm already dressed."

"Begging your pardon, miss, but she's asked me to do your hair and—"

"No. I am already dressed. There is no need for that."

Peggy frowned and gazed at the floor. "May I help you into an evening dress?"

"No. I already dressed for dinner. What I'm wearing is perfectly fine."

"Very good, miss. She'll want you downstairs in a quarter hour." Peggy left, and Elizabeth wondered as she shut the door. What was her mother up to?

In no time at all, Elizabeth stood downstairs in the foyer, awaiting her mother. In honor of the late hour, she donned a dark aubergine-colored cloak and checked her hair in the looking glass in the foyer. Her hair was scraped back into a severe bun, and she wore no earrings, necklaces, or ornaments of any kind.

For an evening party, she would have made an attempt to look presentable and wear a necklace or a comb in her hair, but since the girls at tea had been so rude, she hadn't wanted to dress up. She presented a pretty enough picture, she supposed, although it was strange to be sure, with her mother taking only her to pay an evening call.

Equally dressed in a dark, hooded cloak over her evening gown, and with hardly a word as to where they were going or why, Mrs. Denham took a carriage for her and Elizabeth to Cleveland Row, a better section of town with streetlamps that were well-lit, lighting up the darkness of the night. Then it hit her. This mysterious Mrs. Dove-Lyon might not be holding a party at all.

"Mama? Is this lady very old?"

"Not so much. About my age, I would think. Why?"

"Is she sick?"

"I couldn't say. Why all the questions?"

Elizabeth fretted and twisted a bit of her cloak in her gloved hands, feeling the folds stress and tighten, along with her anxiety. "I'm sorry, Mama. I don't know why I can't seem to make the men like me."

Her mother looked at her.

"But that's no reason to take me to see this woman. I promise you, I can try again. I'll go to as many parties as you like."

"Lizzie?"

"I promise, I don't need to become a companion or live-in nurse to this woman. Honestly, I'll try harder."

Her mother snorted. "Is that what you think?"

"Isn't that why you're bringing me and not Annabelle, or father?"

"Just you wait and see." Her mother laughed, leaned back against the comfortable carriage cushions, and surveyed her daughter with a smile.

She was enjoying this, Elizabeth realized.

"Ah, here we are," her mother said as the carriage pulled to a stop.

With lights shining against the building, Elizabeth could make out it had multiple floors, at least three if not four, and at the front entrance stood a large burly man with military bearing. Mrs. Denham gave their names to the man, who spoke with a servant. In moments their names were checked and confirmed, and they were let in through a side entrance, which Mrs. Denham told Elizabeth was just for the ladies.

"What do you mean? Why aren't we allowed through the front?"

"You'll see. Come along now, we don't want to keep Mrs. Dove-Lyon waiting." They gave their cloaks to a servant and were ushered along by a well-dressed footman through a private entry room and into a pretty sort of parlor, managed by two simply dressed ladies who introduced themselves as Misses Helena and Hermia.

Once given glasses of champagne, they were met by their hostess, Mrs. Dove-Lyon. A woman of middle age, or so Elizabeth guessed, for the woman wore widow's black clothing, complete with jet black jewelry that caught the light, a high-necked dress with smart black buttons, and a delicate black semi-sheer veil that covered her face, but not enough to hide her eyes that sparked with intelligence. It gave her an air of mystery. She was most definitely not an invalid nor a poor, lonely soul in need of a companion.

A kind woman, but one who moved swiftly and with a manner that bespoke of no-nonsense. At a glance, Elizabeth could see she was not to be trifled with. The woman took in the sight of Elizabeth in her faded gown, which was comfortable but did not do her any favors. With her hair pulled back into a severe bun and her skin overly pale, whiter than the delicate rosy-cheeked style so many of the young women fancied, Elizabeth realized she was much less fashionable than her peers.

She had spent her days under the shade of a tree reading, rather than touring the parks or attending picnics out of doors. But that didn't matter. From the pensive purse of Mrs. Dove-Lyon's lips at the sight of her, Elizabeth rather wished she had allowed Peggy to dress her after all.

She sat calmly as her mother and Mrs. Dove-Lyon spoke politely, then her hostess said, "Miss Denham, I would love for you to see more of my house whilst your mother and I talk business. Won't you go explore the salon? Miss Hermia can show you the way."

"Of course." Elizabeth rose and followed the young woman through a dining room where a few women chatted over glasses of wine and plates of roasted lamb before she paused. "They're talking business? What sort of business?"

She turned around, but Miss Hermia said, "I'm sure they'll tell you in good time, Miss Denham. This way."

Elizabeth followed her through to an observation gallery. She stood beside Miss Hermia, a strong, fit woman of average height who moved confidently with the grace of a dancer, or a fighter. She fetched Elizabeth another glass of champagne and said, "Stay here for a bit, Miss."

The first thing that struck her was the noise. She stood on a balcony and below she could see well-dressed men and women talking, laughing, drinking, carousing, dancing, some giggling over cards and games tables, others speaking in tight circles whilst a quartet of musicians played in a corner. It was so loud, Elizabeth could hardly hear over the din, and yet the very sight of it all excited her.

But it was not until a young, dark-haired man turned and stared at her for a full minute, before raising his glass, and she raised her glass in return did she realize aloud, "My God. This isn't just a home, it's a gambling den."

CHAPTER TWO

E LIZABETH WASN'T IN the home of an invalid, or a sickly old woman. Mrs. Dove-Lyon's large home housed a gambling den. This was a far cry from the sedate dining rooms Elizabeth had expected.

Had her mother known when she had taken her there? Was she gambling? But never mind all that. A young man had stared at her, openly and unabashedly, and raised her glass to her in greeting. Who did that? No gentleman, to be sure. And worse, she had toasted him right back. What was wrong with her?

Elizabeth set down her glass immediately. She looked at the man who had caught her eye, then glanced down at her shoes. To stare so boldly at a young man, a stranger, was immodest and most unbecoming in a young woman, she'd been told.

"Miss, do you know that young man?" Miss Hermia asked her.

"Who?"

"That man, there. The one staring at you."

Elizabeth felt a blush warm her cheeks, and peered over the balcony. The man stood, leaning against the edge of a sturdy card table, eyeing her openly.

"No. I don't know who that is," she said.

"I do, and believe me, he is not fit company for a girl like you." A young woman in an ill-fitting pink dress said from behind her, joining them on the balcony. She looked at Elizabeth up and down. "You seem like a sensible sort of girl. I wonder what you are doing here. Are you a teacher? A companion or a governess?"

"No."

"But you look so severe… Oh well, never mind. That man down there is Mr. James. Stay clear of him if you want my advice. He's no good at all. Not for any young woman. How they even let him in here, I do not know."

Miss Hermia shot the woman a level glance and walked away, as Elizabeth asked, "What do you mean?"

The young woman introduced herself as Miss Rowley. She fanned herself with a delicate lace fan and stood beside Elizabeth, glancing down at the men and women chatting and gambling below. "Mr. James is a blackguard, a rake. You'll do good to steer clear of him, mark my words."

"Why?"

Miss Rowley glared at the man until he grinned and stopped staring, then turned his back. Her cheeks reddened and she said, "Because he is a no-good sort of soul. He seduces young women and then once they are ruined, he extorts their families to pay him for his silence."

Elizabeth's eyes grew round. "My word."

"It is true. I would not say it if it were not, you know. It is how he keeps himself in style, by threatening to ruin the young girls' reputations if they do not pay him handsomely."

"How horrible. But he looks so innocent, like a gentleman."

"Hah! Believe me, he is not. Is this your first time here?" Miss Rowley asked.

"Yes. I thought we were attending an evening party, but it seems I was mistaken."

"I thought so too, my first time. But then this is the Lyon's Den, where anything can happen."

"What do you mean?" Elizabeth asked.

They were interrupted by a heavy-set, middle-aged man of military bearing, who bowed and introduced himself as Mr. Flute. He said, "Pardon me for interrupting your conversation. Miss Denham, a gentleman wishes to make your acquaintance."

"Who?" Elizabeth asked. "And how do you know my name?"

Mr. Flute betrayed a small smile. "Mrs. Dove-Lyon always makes us aware of her new guests. Would you allow me to make the introduction?"

"Oh, I bet it's that rake, Mr. James," Miss Rowley said. "Miss Denham, you shouldn't go. The less he knows about you, the better." Seeing her curious expression, she said, "On second thought, you shouldn't go alone. Very well, I'll take you. But be on your guard. The man is a trickster."

Mr. Flute stood in their way. His voice was deep and gravelly. "Forgive me, Miss Rowley, but the gentleman wished to become acquainted with Miss Denham, and her alone."

"Oh." Miss Rowley turned pink as she stood back, allowing Elizabeth to nod to her and follow Mr. Flute through a private room full of ladies laughing and gambling, down a spiral staircase to the main floor, where she briefly became the center of attention.

It was a grand room, the size of a small ballroom, and much of the space was taken up by a small dance floor and a raised area for the musicians to play. Beyond the space for dancing stood small card tables where groups sat and stood about watching games of whist, cribbage, lottery, and piquet. Ladies played hazard and faro, but Elizabeth had little interest in the games. She'd heard one too many stories of ladies losing their fortunes from playing and had no wish to try her luck.

Men glanced at her, and women chatted behind their fans, as Mr.

Flute led the way past a series of gambling tables and guests, to stop before the tall young man who had raised his glass to her earlier.

"Mr. James, allow me to introduce Miss Denham. She is a new guest of Mrs. Dove-Lyon." Mr. Flute stepped aside.

Elizabeth felt all at once alone, conscious that she knew no one, and her mother might as well be on the moon. She glanced at the quickly disappearing form of Mr. Flute, at the tables around them, and then at a polite cough, she gazed up at her new acquaintance.

He was stunningly handsome, but she dared not speak a word of her thoughts aloud, for they were too sinful to be born.

"Miss Denham." He bowed.

"Mr. James." She curtseyed.

"It is a pleasure to meet you," he said. "May I offer you a drink?"

In a moment a servant appeared as if awaiting his signal, and she was given a third glass of champagne. Elizabeth was glad she had eaten a good dinner before, relieved all the alcohol would not go straight to her head. She looked at the man, taking him in.

He wore a blue evening suit, so dark it appeared almost black. He had short black hair, cropped close to his head, expertly cut sideburns, and eyes the shade of midnight. His expression was stern and brooked no nonsense. He looked at her with an intensity that dared to steal her breath away.

She imagined that his smile might outshine the sun, and wondered what it would feel like to have him smile at her.

He asked, "And how are you enjoying the party?"

"I have only just arrived. But it seems like a diverting sort of establishment. Do you come here often?" She asked.

His mouth curled into a smile. "When it suits me. Do you like to play card games?"

"Sometimes. But I'd rather read." The words flew out of her mouth before she could stop them. She bit her lip. Her mother would already be disapproving.

His smile widened. "Indeed? I too enjoy reading, but I do not get a chance to read as often as I would like. What are you reading now?"

She hesitated, then decided he was only being polite, so she might as well be honest. "A book on the Mongols. It's not my favorite part of history, but I am enjoying learning about them." She waited, expecting his eyes to glaze over in boredom.

They didn't.

Instead, they were interrupted by a young man, who wavered on his feet, his shirt and hair rumpled, and he said, slurring his words, "Hello there, you're awfully pretty to be looking so serious. Are you a governess? On a cheeky night out?"

Elizabeth stared at the man. "No." Then she blushed, for the man had spoken to her without being introduced. It was inappropriate and awkward.

Mr. James frowned and took her by the elbow, steering her away from the drunken man. "That man has had too much to drink. Don't mind him. He has forgotten his manners."

"I see." She allowed him to steer her a little way away and asked, "What is your business, Mr. James?"

"My business? You do not think me a gentleman?" He teased.

She blushed. "No, I did not mean that at all. I only meant to enquire whether—"

Miss Rowley sashayed between them, taking Mr. James's arm, and clasping it close to her chest. "Dear Mr. James, fancy seeing you here. I trust you've met our dear Miss Denham, of Denham's Gloves? I've just learnt that her family owns a very good shop in town. I myself bought a pair of kid gloves there off of Bond Street just the other day." She smiled all too sweetly at Elizabeth. "How is your family's business doing?"

Elizabeth colored. "Very well, thank you."

Miss Rowley simpered, and her gloved hands curled around Mr. James's arm tighter. "How nice. Well if you wouldn't mind, Mr. James and I—"

The man in question dropped his arm, pulling away from her. "Miss Rowley, do excuse us. Miss Denham had just agreed to dance with me." He whisked Elizabeth's half-empty champagne flute from her grasp and placed it in Miss Rowley's hands.

Elizabeth stared as Mr. James pulled her firmly away from the others, including Miss Rowley, who gaped at them. Once they were out of earshot Elizabeth asked, "What are you doing?"

"Leading you to the dance floor." He led her to the outskirts of the gambling hall, in the direction of the music.

The musicians were playing a lively tune, comprised of a string, pipe, flute, and drum to keep the beat. A small section of the polished floor had been left empty to accommodate dancers. The floor was mostly empty at the moment, but Mr. James didn't seem to care. He led Elizabeth to the floor and dropped her hand.

He bowed, she curtseyed, and they began to dance. In no time at all other couples joined them and soon they danced in a circle, changing partners and moving in a simple quadrille. As they danced together, she asked, "Why did you do that? Miss Rowley seemed put out."

"I do not like those who seek to put down others."

She continued dancing. Once it ended, he joined her off to the side of the floor as more couples began a new set.

She said quietly, "It is all right, you know. My family being in trade is not shameful to me. And I would not keep the acquaintance of anyone who thought less of me for it."

He looked at her. "Fine words, Miss Denham." He added, "There are many here who would overlook a humbler situation in life if it meant being able to pay their bills on time. Were you to peek into their account ledgers, you would find a number of patrons who are enjoying themselves on credit."

"Sounds like a precarious situation to me," she said.

"It is. There are some in this room who play cards and drink and hope to earn a bit to pay their way, but it is never enough. It is all too easy to lose sense of themselves, of law and decorum, and to play dangerously, putting their houses, their servants, everything they have on the line for a bit of chance."

"Is it worth it?" she asked.

"No. But I think you will also find that if you spoke with some of the men and women here, they would know little of the history of past cultures and spend their efforts on finding the latest fashions or scandals amongst their acquaintance."

"Hmmm." Elizabeth remembered Miss Rowley's words and wondered if they were true.

"What are you thinking?" he asked. "Do you dislike my company? I am a mere gentleman, so perhaps you would prefer I introduce you to a lord or entitled aristocrat?"

She laughed. "No doubt my mother would say yes. But I don't mind the present company." She blushed.

The corners of his eyes crinkled in delight. "Then we are in agreement."

They stood by as Miss Rowley circulated around the room, speaking with gentlemen and ladies, then shooting little darting glances at her.

"I think Miss Rowley is talking about me," Elizabeth said. "She thought I was a governess when we first met."

"I suspect she thinks that in besmirching your good name and relaying your family's profession, she will undermine you in the presence of others."

Elizabeth tensed. Would her visit at Mrs. Dove-Lyon's be of a short duration?

Mr. James continued, "But she forgets herself, and worse, only does herself harm in their eyes," he said, leading her into the next dance, a country reel.

"How so?" she asked, soon breathless.

"Any real gentleman or member of the ton will seek to make their own mind up, rather than trust the gossiping tongue of a poor gentleman's daughter."

"You think?"

He did not answer but she observed closely and indeed, Miss Rowley's hair was dressed fashionably, but that was all that could be said. Her gown was two years out of date, at least, and looked old. Her gloves did not match her dress and were ill-fitting, and she had the harried expression of a woman on an ill-fated mission, rather than out to enjoy herself, if her expression were any indication.

"I had thought her kind," Elizabeth said, then looked at him. "What is your relationship with Miss Rowley?"

He breathed in noisily. "I once saved her from an imprudent marriage. Her family was most grateful. But when she aimed to replace her suitor with myself, that put us both in an awkward position."

"Oh."

"I would rather not discuss the particulars, if it's all the same to you, Miss Denham. There are better things to talk about and prettier partners than Miss Rowley." He looked her in the eye as the dance came to an end. He held her hand, and for a moment, she thought she could hear her heart beating. But was it from the dancing, or excitement at his touch?

"Elizabeth, there you are. Come away dear, we've stayed here long enough." Her mother stood by, flanked by Miss Hermia. "And who is your friend? A new acquaintance?"

He dropped her hand. She turned and faced her mother. "Mama, do allow me to present Mr. James."

"A pleasure, madam." He bowed. To Elizabeth, he murmured, "Miss Denham, we will have to continue our dance another time. I would not let go of a bewitching partner so easily."

Elizabeth curtseyed and rose as he took her hand.

His eyes sought hers and for a second it seemed he might not let go. He held her hand a second longer than necessary, meeting her gaze with his own. "We will speak again, Miss Denham. Good evening."

She nodded, feeling a blush come to her cheeks. "Good night, Mr. James."

CHAPTER THREE

T HE FOLLOWING NIGHT, Mrs. Denham took Elizabeth to the
Lyon's Den again, but this time kept by her side as they entered
the main room.

That evening, Elizabeth wore a sky-blue dress with a low, scooped
bodice, trimmed in gold thread and with a thin, gold sash around her
high empire waist. Her dark hair was swept in a sensible bun, but
having let Peggy dress her hair, the simple style was now adorned with
a gold ribbon tied around her hair like a Greek muse. The effect was
pretty enough, she supposed.

The strains of violins and a pipe swelled and filled the room, and
Elizabeth and her mother chatted with several ladies, whilst adeptly
avoiding Miss Rowley, who soon disappeared upstairs.

"Who was that young woman who kept shooting you dirty
looks?" Mrs. Denham asked, joining a card game.

"That is a Miss Rowley."

"And what have you done to make her dislike you?" Her mother
missed nothing.

"She views me as a rival, I think. And she disapproves of Father's
profession," Elizabeth said quietly.

Her mother froze, sitting stiff as a poker. An unobservant person might not notice anything amiss, but to anyone that knew the Denham family, they might spy the slight curl of her hand, the subtle stiffness of her body and the way she sat, down to the narrowing of her eyes and sudden pursing of her lips. Mrs. Denham knew very well what some people might think of their background as a family in trade, but she would be damned if they mistreated her daughter for it.

After turning over a card, Mrs. Denham asked, "And where is the gentleman you were speaking with the other night?"

"Mr. James?"

"Yes. He seemed like an amiable fellow."

As if saying his name conjured him like magic, he appeared and bowed, taking Elizabeth's hand. Tonight, he wore a slate gray waistcoat and breeches, a deep russet waistcoat with embroidered thread that caught the light, over a crisp white cravat. His dark hair was tousled as if a woman had just run her fingers through it, and unlike so many of the men, he was not clean shaven, and instead bore the traces of a light fuzz around his chin. It gave him a roguish appeal that earned many admiring glances from the ladies present.

"Miss Denham, Mrs. Denham. A pleasure to see you here again." He spoke the words, but looked only at Elizabeth.

"Hello, Mr. James," she said.

He smiled and their eyes locked, trapped in a mutual gaze. If her mother spoke, Elizabeth did not hear.

Mr. James acquired glasses of champagne for her and her mother and then led Elizabeth to one of the gambling tables, where a dealer was dealing out cards. Elizabeth had little interest in card games, and her attention was soon diverted by Miss Rowley and a young man who walked down the side stairs and entered the main gambling hall. It did not surprise her to see Miss Rowley acting so informally with a young man, but her hands were entwined around the man's arm so tightly, it seemed almost possessive.

Elizabeth asked, "What is in the upper rooms, upstairs?"

Mr. James quirked an eyebrow, his eyes amused. "Do you really wish to know?"

"Miss Rowley and her companion have just come from there. Although he looks familiar somehow..." She gasped. "I know that gentleman. That's Mr. Hickson."

Mr. James's eyebrows rose.

"I mean, I met him the other day at the Plimpetts'. We had tea together."

"And was he a brilliant conversationalist?"

"Not at all. He rather disliked me correcting him on his history. But Mr. James, he is to be engaged to Miss Plimpett. What is he doing in the company of Miss Rowley?"

He glanced over at the laughing couple and shrugged. "If they have come from upstairs, then they were perhaps enjoying each other's better acquaintance."

"What do you mean?"

"Are you really so naive?" he asked.

They looked at each other, he in amusement, she in confusion. "They're making their better acquaintance... I... Oh. You mean..."

A corner of his mouth quirked in a smile. "The upper rooms are available for purchase, for an hour or two. If Mrs. Dove-Lyon allows it."

Elizabeth's mouth dropped open. "Oh." She looked away. "I thought this a respectable sort of place."

"It is, to a point. Rumor has it that when Mrs. Dove-Lyon's husband died, there was nothing but debts. Mrs. Dove-Lyon had an idea to go into business for herself and has done remarkably well. But part of that success is down to her ability for discretion. There is no one here who has not been invited or discreetly observed and assessed by the good lady herself before being allowed inside," he said.

"But for Miss Rowley to do such a thing under this roof, especially when Mr. Hickson is about to be engaged to another girl…"

"It is possible they did not use the upper rooms for that purpose at all. It may be that he has not told Miss Rowley, and she thinks it an innocent dalliance. Perhaps they are engaged themselves, and your friend Miss Plimpett has yet to find out," he told her. "It might be completely innocent."

"Do you think so?" she asked.

"Honestly? No. In my experience, things are often as they appear." He nodded to a table near them, where a large woman and another man with military bearing stood playing cards. "Take them, for instance. The good lady, Mrs. Alfreda Beaumont. You see that large gem around her neck?"

"Yes." A large garnet, as big as a robin's egg, hung around her neck on a silken ribbon, and was surrounded by other small diamonds that winked in the candlelight.

Mrs. Beaumont herself was a large woman, with curled gray hair. She wore a tight dress the color of burnt sienna, her round bodice trimmed with many miniature ruffles and bows. She wore fine elbow gloves and carried a fan, but the stunning garnet around her neck was the clear attraction. Mrs. Beaumont carried herself with a smart confidence and warm laugh and gave the impression of being quite jolly. But soon, Mrs. Beaumont's attention was sought by Miss Rowley and Mr. Hickson, as well as a few other gentlemen.

Elizabeth finished her drink and took two from a passing footman to hand to Mr. James. As she handed him a glass, he touched her index finger with his as he accepted it. She froze for a second. Had it been an accident or intentional? She looked at him.

He gazed back at her as if attempting to seem innocent, but he failed at this, and only appeared serious and calculating. She repressed a nervous shiver and opened her mouth to speak when a cry rent the air.

Mrs. Beaumont crashed to the floor. A strangled sound could be heard.

"My god, she's fallen," Mr. James said, setting aside their drinks. He and Elizabeth hurried toward the woman.

People surrounded Mrs. Beaumont, including servants, Mr. Flute, and Miss Hermia, as well as Mrs. Dove-Lyon herself. "What has happened?" she asked.

"The lady's fainted, help me," Mr. Hickson said, crushed beneath Mrs. Beaumont on the floor.

"Give her some room," Mr. James said, urging people to move back.

"Oh my, Mrs. Beaumont, Mrs. Beaumont, can you hear me?" Miss Rowley cradled her head in her lap as Mr. Hickson moved out from beneath her, brushing himself off.

People stood back, and a man pushed through the crowd. "I am a doctor, let me through." An older gentleman dressed in evening dress entered the small space and knelt by her. He quickly assessed her for injuries. "Mrs. Dove-Lyon, do you have any smelling salts?"

"I have some," a dealer said, reaching for a small vial inside his sleeve. "For emergencies." He handed the vial over.

"Thank you." The doctor took the vial and held it beneath Mrs. Beaumont's nose. Within a few seconds, the woman's eyelids fluttered, and she breathed, "Oh my. What happened? Did I fall?"

"You fainted, madam." The doctor helped her sit up. "How are you feeling?"

"Hot. I feel very warm. Perhaps I might go outside for some fresh air?" she asked.

"A very wise idea. I will escort you." The doctor said, and helped her up. He returned the smelling salts to the dealer and said, "A glass of brandy would help."

But as they began to walk from the gaming table, Mrs. Beaumont froze. She patted her neck and looked down in dismay. "My necklace," Mrs. Beaumont cried. "It's gone!"

People soon surrounded her. Mrs. Beaumont fretted and looked around. "Where is it? My necklace, my beautiful garnet…"

People began to search, looking along the floor and around the gaming tables, but it was nowhere to be seen. "It couldn't have gone far," one person said.

"Aye, the bloody thing was huge," another guest agreed.

"I think it's been stolen." Mrs. Beaumont's voice carried. "Someone has taken my garnet."

Mrs. Dove-Lyon looked up in alarm. She turned and with a single glance and a nod to the footmen at the entrances, the doors closed.

"What is the meaning of this?" a gentleman asked her.

"Just a precaution, Mr. White. If Mrs. Beaumont's necklace has gone missing, this will make sure it doesn't leave the building."

"You don't really think one of us took it, do you?" he asked.

Mrs. Dove-Lyon shrugged. "Whilst they are under my roof, I take the property of my guests very seriously, sir. If Mrs. Beaumont's necklace has disappeared, I want to make sure we find it."

Elizabeth watched this exchange with interest when Mrs. Dove-Lyon approached them. "Ah, Mr. James, Miss Denham. I wonder if perhaps you two might look into this matter?"

Elizabeth's eyebrows rose. "You want us to help?"

"Yes, if you wouldn't mind. Your mother has told me of your inquisitiveness, and I thought with your education and Mr. James's skills, you might discover its whereabouts before any unpleasantness happens."

"We will gladly help," Mr. James said, giving a fractional nod to Elizabeth.

"Excellent. All I can tell you is that none of my servants would have done such a thing. I pay them well and they are above reproach," Mrs. Dove-Lyon said.

"That means, then, it really has gone missing or one of the guests took it," Elizabeth said.

"Yes. Now, when Mrs. Beaumont fell, I noticed just a handful of people around her. The dealer, Mr. Hickson, Miss Rowley, Colonel Jeffries, and Miss Dawkins. I imagine one of them might know something, or have stolen it themselves," their hostess said.

"What can you tell us about them?" Mr. James asked.

"Mr. Hickson is newly arrived in town, but rumor has it he is about to become engaged to a young lady, with an income of five thousand a year. Miss Rowley is a regular guest of ours, who I believe is acquainted with yourself."

"And the others?" he asked.

"The colonel I have known for some time. He comes here often as not and likes a good game. I believe him to be completely trustworthy. Miss Dawkins is new to my establishment. I know little about her, other than she is looking for a husband." Mrs. Dove-Lyon looked at Elizabeth. "Good luck. Please hurry. I do not know how long I can honestly keep the doors closed without causing a scene. If you do not find out who did this, my business will suffer." She left them in a swish of black skirts.

"Let us ask them together," Mr. James suggested.

"Good idea."

They approached Miss Rowley first, who fanned herself and took a drink of champagne from a passing footman. "Oh, it's you." She did not curtsey and focused her attention on Mr. James, at whom she flashed a smile.

"I wonder, Miss Rowley, if you happened to notice anything when Mrs. Beaumont fell?" Mr. James asked.

"Me? No, not really. Are you looking into this matter, then?" She set down her fan and trailed a hand on Mr. James's arm.

"Yes."

"Well once the old lady fell, I did what I could to support her. But I didn't see anyone take her necklace and don't know what happened. Do you really think someone took it?"

"It's possible," Elizabeth said.

Miss Rowley didn't even dignify her presence with a look. Instead, she leaned in close to Mr. James and said, "If you must know, I think that young woman, Miss Dawkins, took it. She's from a poor family in trade, and hasn't much to say for herself. I saw her eyeing the woman's necklace earlier; she couldn't take her eyes off of it. She's probably wondering how much she could sell it for. If I had to guess, I would suspect her a thief."

"And you have no other proof of her guilt, other than her background?" Elizabeth asked.

That earned a sweet smile from Miss Rowley. "It's such a shame when establishments let in just anyone. I mean, this used to be a place where good families came to socialize but now, it seems anyone with enough money could walk in. It's all well and good I suppose, but inviting in the wrong sort rather brings down the quality of the place, don't you think?"

Elizabeth fumed and held her tongue.

"Thank you, Miss Rowley." Mr. James gently disengaged her hand from his arm and led Elizabeth away. "Hold your temper," he said quietly.

"She doesn't make it easy," Elizabeth said.

"You're above her jibes and she knows it. Keep a level head, Miss Denham. Our hostess would not have asked you to be included in this investigation if she did not think highly of your abilities."

"That is very kind of you to say," Elizabeth said.

"It is true."

Once in front of the young woman in question, Elizabeth began the conversation. "Miss Dawkins?"

The young woman couldn't have been more than twenty years old, but seemed younger. Her eyes widened and she jumped like a church mouse. "Oh, hello. It's very exciting, this theft, isn't it?"

From Miss Dawkins's wide-eyed excitement and youthful blush of her cheeks to Mr. James's forced smile, she could tell that he was unimpressed with her youth.

"Yes, it is. We're investigating this matter for Mrs. Dove-Lyon. Did you happen to see anything odd?" he asked.

"What, when the grand lady fell? No. Nothing really. It was so exciting; I didn't really notice much. Although I wonder, is that young man a doctor?" She nodded toward Mr. Hickson.

"No, I don't believe so. Why?"

"Well, it was just he had a good presence of mind to instruct that girl to hold Mrs. Beaumont's head when she fell, just like a nurse I'd imagine. It made me wonder if he was a surgeon or something."

"Who do you imagine took Mrs. Beaumont's necklace?" Elizabeth asked.

"Oh, definitely a man, for sure."

"Why is that?" Mr. James asked.

Miss Dawkins held up her arms and turned around in a circle, her light brown dress swinging around her shapely form. "You see?"

"It is a very pretty dress," Mr. James said.

Miss Dawkins laughed. "It is not that, sir. It is that we have nowhere to put such things. Our dresses have no pockets, you see. That necklace looked so big; I could see it from across the room. I do like pretty things, but I'd never know how to take a necklace like that if I were a thief, or where to put it."

Miss Dawkins left them then, offering a shy smile at Mr. James as she left.

Elizabeth murmured, "I think that young lady has taken a fancy to you."

"What a shame it is not reciprocated."

"Is there no lady that has taken your eye?" she teased.

"Perhaps. Are we such good acquaintances to share our confidences with each other?" he asked, a slight smile on his face.

"After an evening or two? I think not," she said, looking away.

"What a pity. Never mind. You will just have to wonder at the identity of the lady who has caught my eye."

"Is she pretty?" Elizabeth asked.

"Very," he said.

"Smart?"

"Absolutely."

They looked at each other, when he said, "Let us speak with the colonel."

Upon introducing themselves to the colonel, the older gentleman said, "Speculating about who's stolen the gem, eh? Well, you're wasting your time. I wager it's that woman who's gone and done it."

"Who?" Mr. James asked.

"The old dame herself, Beaumont. I've known her for a long time and she's getting on in years. She's always losing things. I bet she thought she'd put on the necklace tonight and forgot to put it on. When she goes home tonight, she'll find it sitting on her dresser, mark my words," the colonel said.

Elizabeth looked at Mr. James with slight dismay. Could their search have been for nothing?

Mr. James said, "Ah, but sir, a few of the people here remarked at seeing it. I do believe the lady was wearing it when she entered this room."

Colonel Jeffries coughed delicately. "Oh. Well then. Dashed if I know."

"Does the lady have any enemies?" Elizabeth asked. "Someone who might try to steal it?"

"Not that I know of. Mrs. Beaumont is a kind soul. Perhaps not everyone's cup of tea, but she wouldn't hurt a fly. No one in their right mind would want to rob her. She's the sweetest woman you'll ever meet. Now if you'll excuse me, I must speak to her." He left them.

"What about the doctor?" Mr. James asked Elizabeth. "He was close to Mrs. Beaumont once she had fainted, and he would have been in close proximity to her, enough so he could have removed the necklace."

"But by that time everyone was watching. How could he have done it with such a wide audience?" Elizabeth asked. "And also, how successful a doctor could he be if he goes around stealing from his patients?"

"Fair point. My gut tells me he is new to the establishment. I've certainly never seen him before." Mr. James scratched his chin. "That could of course, go either in his favor or not."

Elizabeth glanced across the room, to where the doctor was consoling Mrs. Beaumont with a glass of strong brandy.

"I'm not sure it was him. If he was a thief, surely he would try to distance himself from her as soon as possible, rather than stay by her side," she said.

"Unless he is putting up a very good front. It is possible."

She looked at him. "Now what? We're no closer to finding out who did this than before," Elizabeth said.

"Aren't we? Think about what we know," he said.

She considered the facts. "We know it is unlikely the colonel took it, as he thought she'd forgotten to put the necklace on in the first place. Miss Dawkins thinks a man must have done it as women's clothes today have no pockets, so that eliminates Miss Rowley and herself, whilst the dealer is above suspicion, which only leaves Mr. Hickson."

"But he wasn't in a position to remove the necklace from Mrs. Beaumont. The only person who was close enough to do that was…"

"My goodness," Elizabeth said, understanding.

Mrs. Dove-Lyon approached them. "I say, sorry to hurry you along, but are you any closer to finding out the thief? Mrs. Beaumont is most distressed, and the doctor says she needs fresh air. I need to open the doors before the room becomes stifling." She paused, "And if you do not figure this out, I will need to call the watch. I do not wish to, but…"

"Do not trouble yourself, Mrs. Dove-Lyon," Mr. James said. "We know who did it."

"You do?"

"Yes," Elizabeth said.

"Who?" Miss Rowley asked, coming up to them.

"Yes, indeed, tell us," the colonel said.

In seconds, Mr. James and Elizabeth found themselves the center of attention. Mr. James cleared his throat. "It became clear to us that out of the people here, the person who stole the necklace had a quick moment to take the opportunity. In the confusion, there was only one person who could have taken it."

"Who?" a few people asked.

"Miss Denham, if you would?" Mr. James asked.

All eyes were on her as she spoke, "The person who stole the necklace is… Miss Rowley."

"What?" The colonel said.

"No," Mrs. Dove-Lyon said. "It can't be."

"It's true," Elizabeth said.

"You are mistaken." Miss Rowley laughed. "I should have known you would stoop to this. You're such a bluestocking, my goodness. But then your family is in trade, so of course you would try to pin this on me." Her voice carried. "This girl has tried to make me the brunt of her jokes since she arrived. All because she is jealous of me."

People looked at Elizabeth, who blushed at being the center of attention. She said in a faltering voice, "What Miss Rowley says is untrue."

"Oh really? Then tell me, where is the necklace now?" Miss Rowley held up her arms. "You can search me if you like, I haven't got it."

"We know. That's because you gave it to your lover, Mr. Hickson," Mr. James said.

Mr. Hickson jerked and tugged at his messily tied cravat. "Me?

What? No. You're wrong. I'd never do such a thing. And we aren't… um… You know." His cheeks turned pink, as did Miss Rowley's.

Mr. James said, "Check his pockets. The girl passed it to him in the confusion and he's been waiting for the doors to open to make his escape. Miss Dawkins thought it odd he had instructed Miss Rowley to hold Mrs. Beaumont's head, and wondered if he was a doctor, but as he isn't, it's very strange. It would have given her the perfect opportunity to remove the necklace. Once the doctor arrived, Miss Rowley would have found it easy to slip it to him in the group of people."

"Oi, don't touch me," Mr. Hickson protested as two of the footmen accosted him. One held his arms behind his back whilst another checked his pockets and his inner waistcoat. "There's nothing here."

Mr. Hickson stumbled away, limping. "See? I'm innocent."

"Why are you limping, Mr. Hickson?" Elizabeth asked.

"That woman fell on me when she fainted. Damn near broke my legs," he said rudely, earning a gasp from Mrs. Beaumont.

"Check his legs," Mr. James said.

"Oi, get your hands off me!" he said.

The footman patted down Mr. Hickson, and there, in his knee-length boots, was an odd sound. The footman glanced at Mr. Hickson and removed his boot, revealing the garnet necklace to come tumbling out. It winked in the candlelight, shining brilliantly for all to see.

People gasped, whispered, and stared at the sight of it, next to Mr. Hickson's foot, which looked particularly bad since his sock had an unsightly hole in the toe. He scowled as Mrs. Dove-Lyon said, "Take him out of here. I won't tolerate stealing."

"It was all a jape, it was, honest, Mrs. Dove-Lyon," Mr. Hickson said, as the pair of footmen held him fast. "Honest to goodness it was. Miss Rowley just wanted to see if I could fetch her something pretty, and I told her I could. We wagered on it. I bet her I could steal the necklace off that woman's neck, and she didn't believe me. It was just a joke, I would have returned it in no time."

"A likely story," Elizabeth commented.

He glared at her and turned to Mrs. Beaumont. "It was just a little prank, that is all. I never meant to harm you, good lady. We were going to return the necklace as soon as possible. I just didn't get the chance because this bluestocking started poking her nose around in it like it was a real crime."

"It was real," Elizabeth said.

Miss Rowley shook her head. "My dear Miss Denham, when will you learn? This is the Lyon's Den, where people bet on everything. You are far too naive, I think, to understand the difference between truth and fiction. This was a harmless prank between friends. And to think, you truly alarmed poor Mrs. Beaumont." She plucked the necklace from the floor and handed it to the woman. "Here you are, Mrs. Beaumont. So sorry to have troubled you."

Elizabeth felt embarrassed. Mr. James stood beside her as Mrs. Dove-Lyon said, "This may have been a joke, but I take such matters very seriously."

"I apologize," Mr. Hickson said.

"It was an honest mistake. Just a little joke between friends, I'm sure." Mrs. Beaumont took the necklace and had it put back on by the colonel, who offered her his arm. She smiled benevolently at all, but her smile faded as she whispered to the colonel, who promptly escorted her from the room. With the doors now opened, fresh air entered the hall, and many people left, leaving only a handful inside. Miss Rowley and Mr. Hickson quit the room quickly, arm in arm, but not before shooting poisonous glares at Elizabeth.

Mrs. Dove-Lyon shook her head. "What a mess. Mr. James, Miss Denham, please join me for a drink." She led them through the hall into a private salon decorated with black chairs and pink cushions, matching a warm pink wallpaper. The effect was curious. She bade them sit and closed the door, pouring them each a glass of brandy. "What an evening. I'm indebted to you, Mr. James, and you, Miss

Denham, for finding out who was behind that. I'm sure you appreciate the gravity of the situation as well as I do."

Elizabeth nodded and quietly sipped her brandy. It was strong and made her cough.

Mrs. Dove-Lyon gave a level look as she said, "Needless to say, this sort of thing cannot happen again. A game is one thing, but this could all have ended very differently. Had Mrs. Beaumont not been so gracious about their little wager, I don't want to think about how differently this could have ended."

"You cannot think it was actually a game," Elizabeth said.

"I think Miss Rowley flattered Mr. Hickson, and he made her a bet he could steal her Mrs. Beaumont's necklace. I have no doubt they truly planned to take it and leave," Mrs. Dove-Lyon said.

"Thanks to your quick thinking they didn't, ma'am," Mr. James said.

Mrs. Dove-Lyon inclined her head. "Thank you. Like I said, I am indebted to you. Which is why I propose the following. Miss Denham, you were called a bluestocking tonight."

Elizabeth looked down at her brandy. "I know."

"Are you bothered by it?"

Elizabeth gazed at the floor, then met her hostess's eyes. "A little. I am bookish, so I do not mind. But they made it sound like being educated was a bad thing. And it is not."

"Quite right. But I have observed you and spoken with your mother. Do you know why she brought you here?" Mrs. Dove-Lyon said.

Elizabeth shook her head.

"She hopes that you might find a man here and entice him to marriage."

Elizabeth's mouth dropped open. "What? In a gambling den? Why?" Her cheeks bloomed pink.

Mrs. Dove-Lyon smiled. "I suspect she reached the conclusion that as you have so far been unable to make a match with a suitable gentleman, she is willing to place you in the vicinity of those who are somewhat… less scrupulous in their choice of bride."

"I say," Mr. James said. "That's a bit much, ma'am."

"Is it? The girl talks of little else but history and the Mongols. It would take more than an ordinary gentleman to tolerate that sort of eccentricity, even with her dowry, not to mention her looks."

"What is wrong with my looks?" Elizabeth asked.

"Nothing," Mr. James said firmly.

"Ahem," Mrs. Dove-Lyon said. "You were also asked whether you were a governess, yes?"

"What does that have to do with anything? Oh. I see," Elizabeth said. "You think I am too severe."

"It is a look you have affected; I suspect unconsciously so. You have a classic, natural beauty, but you seem intent on hiding it behind a severe appearance." At Elizabeth's protest she raised a finger. "I was making a statement of fact, not asking a question."

"What is the meaning of this, Mrs. Dove-Lyon?" Mr. James's voice was curt, earning him a look from his hostess.

"I propose the following. Mr. James, you are a connoisseur of female beauty, and have graced many a salon in your time."

He raised a roguish eyebrow at this. "You make it sound like I am fifty, not twenty-seven."

"Miss Denham, you are in need of a few alterations to your appearance and conversation. Your natural grace and temperament are fine, but you will need to learn the fine art of conversation if you are to attract and retain a man. Your mother has promised to pay highly for me to find you an eligible man to marry."

Elizabeth squeezed her brandy tumbler, feeling the fragile glass in her fingers, and set it on the floor. She rested her hands on her knees and ended up gripping them instead. "I have no need of your services. I can do very well on my own. When I am ready." She rose to her feet.

"Please Miss Denham, sit down. I do not mean to be insulting, only matter of fact. You are twenty-five, are you not?"

Elizabeth blushed and sat. "Twenty-two."

"My mistake. Your appearance suggested you were older." Mrs. Dove-Lyon frowned. "The fact is that your family are beginning to despair of you ever making a suitable match."

Elizabeth opened her mouth to protest, when Mrs. Dove-Lyon held up a hand. "Forgive my frankness, Miss Denham, I only repeat the impression I was given by your mother, and what I have observed yesterday and tonight. I propose the following. During the daytime, these rooms are somewhat empty. Come in and allow me to assist you with your dress, and Mr. James will teach you the ways of conversation that will attract a man."

Elizabeth looked at the floor. "You make it sound like I am a lost cause."

"Not at all. I give it a week, maybe two, before you find someone."

The idea of parading herself around like a piece of trussed-up cattle at a market made her feel low. As if she had nothing to offer but the fine quality of her dress, her gloves, her fair complexion, and her teeth. She asked, "Do I have a choice?"

"Yes. But I will say, your mother is happy to pay for this service. Out of respect for the reputational damage you have saved me tonight, I am willing to waive that fee, for now."

Elizabeth looked at Mr. James. "And you, sir, you are willing to teach me? So I might attract a suitor?"

He nodded, his dark eyes serious. "If that is what you want."

"Is there anything I can do in return?" she asked.

He coughed and turned pink. Mrs. Dove-Lyon cocked her head and shot her a dubious look, when Mr. James cleared his throat. "I have an idea. I know nothing of history. I read the paper but know little of ancient cultures. Perhaps... Miss Denham could teach me a few things. So that I might know what she is talking about. For our

41

conversation lessons."

"Excellent idea. Miss Denham? What do you say?" Mrs. Dove-Lyon asked.

"All right." Elizabeth picked up her brandy, drank, and coughed again before setting it down.

"Mr. James will see you out. Thank you again, for catching the thieves," Mrs. Dove-Lyon said.

Mr. James offered Elizabeth his arm and escorted her to the entrance of the ladies' private gambling rooms. "Are you sure you are open to this arrangement?" he asked.

"To be honest, I'm not sure. I feel deceived somewhat by my mother. But at the same time, I wouldn't mind learning to converse with a man without him thinking I am a governess. I don't want to be a spinster, or dismissed as a bluestocking."

"There is nothing wrong with being a bluestocking," he said.

"You are too kind, Mr. James. But I am already getting tired of the name. I shall look forward to our lessons," she said with a smile.

"As will I." He took her hand and held it again, for a second longer, before letting go.

As he escorted her back to her mother, Elizabeth's mind wandered. What was happening to her? Was she really going to enter into this arrangement, all to find a man? The independent woman inside her railed against this with every fiber of her being.

"What is it, Miss Denham?" he asked.

"Just that it feels a sorry thing for me to have been educated and to develop a love of learning, only to find it considered unattractive. And that in order to find a man, I need to display my family's wealth and my own physical assets. And for what? To bear a child. Have a family and eventually grow old and die. Surely myself and other young women must have more purpose than that."

He smiled. "You take a very dim view of a woman's place in the world, do you realize that? And it is not all as bad as you say. Some men and women enjoy the chase, the hunt of finding a suitable partner. You never know. You might find attracting a husband to be enjoyable."

"Hah." She snorted, but the knowing look in his eyes made her blush. What was he going on about?

She had not been educated just to bear children. But a more diplomatic side won out. "We'll just have to see, Mr. James."

CHAPTER FOUR

THE NEXT DAY Elizabeth brought her sister Annabelle to the den and was ushered into a private room, where Mrs. Dove-Lyon and an assistant, Miss Leigh, a thin, red-haired young woman, with a slight trace of a French accent, immediately assessed them with pursed lips and narrowed eyes.

The room had decent windows which let in the sunlight, revealing trim curtains and bright yellow wallpaper of a paisley design, which looked rather expensive to Elizabeth's eye. The room was lightly furnished with a few chairs and in the center of the room, a small round pedestal. Elizabeth had seen something similar in a dressmaker's shop, and wondered idly if her dresses needed altering.

Annabelle stood apart as Mrs. Dove-Lyon made the introductions. The girls exchanged a look as Miss Leigh surveyed them both, her lips pursed.

"You." She addressed Annabelle and circled her, noting her light pink dress. "You are very good. Excellent taste, oui. I could do little."

Annabelle grinned. "Thank you."

"You may go."

"Oh, but I'm here. That's my sister."

Miss Leigh shrugged and gestured for Elizabeth to stand upon the pedestal. Once she did, the woman hemmed and hmmmed, looking her up and down. "Who dressed you?"

"My maidservant," Elizabeth said.

Miss Leigh frowned. "That color is hideous. Do not wear it ever again. Please, take it off."

Elizabeth looked at her pretty purple dress. It was a bit faded, and the embroidered threads of the flowers had gotten slightly frayed, but it was comfortable, and she liked it. "But I like this dress."

"Wear it at home, where no one but you can see it. Please, take it off. It offends me," Miss Leigh said, looking pointedly away from Elizabeth's dress.

Elizabeth balked. "But I have nothing else to wear. Mrs. Dove-Lyon, really, is this necessary? Must I?"

"Your mother is paying for my help, Miss Denham," Mrs. Dove-Lyon said. "It would be a shame to waste it."

"Come on, Lizzie, might as well humor her," Annabelle whispered to her.

"Very well."

"I will find something." Miss Leigh turned to Mrs. Dove-Lyon, who nodded and quit the room.

Annabelle helped Elizabeth out of the dress, until she stood in her stays, plain shift, white stockings, and shoes. Elizabeth shivered and crossed her arms beneath her chest.

"Your hair…" Miss Leigh stepped forward and in a matter of seconds, had removed the pins that had held Elizabeth's severe bun, freeing her rippling dark hair into a style that befitted a mermaid.

It was of course at that minute, that Mr. James knocked and entered the room. He froze and his eyes widened. "Miss Denham."

Elizabeth jumped and squeaked. She jumped from the platform and ducked behind her sister Annabelle, who was shorter. The effect of sisterly camouflage failed on a grand scale, much to Mr. James's amusement.

"Mr. James," Elizabeth said, blushing. "Turn your back."

He turned around.

Elizabeth noticed it was a very nice back. He wore beige trousers, a forest green waistcoat and matching beige suit jacket with a lightly tied cravat. His hair looked tousled and damp, as if he'd recently had a bath and run his fingers through his hair. A part of her wondered what he smelled like, and she swallowed, banishing the thought.

She could hear the amusement in his voice. "Are you all right, Miss Denham? You seem to have lost your dress."

"She is fine. I am helping her," Miss Leigh said.

"By stripping her of her clothes? Not that I mind, but I imagine she might make many new friends tonight if she were to attend the main hall dressed just like that."

"I am not going out without a dress," Elizabeth said.

"Of course not. You just need to wear the right dress. Not what you had on," Miss Leigh said.

"I understand," Elizabeth said, through slightly gritted teeth.

Mr. James chuckled. "I suppose I am too early for my history lesson?"

Annabelle snorted, as Elizabeth shifted her feet, covering herself with her hands. "Mr. James, if you would kindly leave us…"

He held up a hand. "I'm going. Forgive the intrusion. When you are decent, Miss Denham, I will be waiting for you downstairs." He quit the room.

Mrs. Dove-Lyon reentered the room and began discussing the merits of a handful of dresses she had brought in with Miss Leigh. Whilst they examined Elizabeth's height and skin tone against the options, Annabelle turned and said, "That man likes you."

"What?"

"Mr. James. Who is he? I think he fancies you."

"You are mistaken." Elizabeth looked away.

"I'm not. I have an eye for style, and I know when a man likes a woman. He likes you."

"Don't be ridiculous."

Annabelle shrugged as Mrs. Dove-Lyon and Miss Leigh chose a dress of white satin with a fine gauzy muslin petticoat over it, with a dark forest green bodice made of satin with small cap sleeves, trimmed with a silver border. Despite her lack of interest in ladies' fashion, Elizabeth could tell the gown was beautiful.

Once she was wearing it, she felt beautiful.

"Now we just need to fix your hair," Miss Leigh commented.

In no time at all, Elizabeth's severe, pared back bun was changed into a braided design. Still a bun, but less like a school mistress, this time with a pearl comb in her hair. With a pearl necklace at her throat and a pair of light white kid gloves, she felt rather like royalty.

Elizabeth, now suitably dressed, walked down the spiral back staircase that led from the ladies' observation balcony to the back of the main gambling hall. As she opened the door, a regular flood of noise filled her ears, as the strains of the musicians playing combined with the chatter and laughter of men and women present gambling.

She began to walk around one of the tables and spotted Mr. James standing by with a drink. He handed her a glass of wine and said, "You found a dress, I see."

"Yes." Elizabeth shot him a level look and earned a snort from him. "So, tell me, Mr. James, what would you like to know about history?"

And the lessons began. Over wine she told him about the ancient Greeks and Romans, and the famous Helen of Troy, from Homer's *Iliad*. The next evening over cards she informed him of the medieval knights, and the warring armies of King Stephen and Queen Matilda, versus the Empress Matilda in the twelfth century. Over games of chess and hazard, she told him of the Mongols, the crusades, the stories of Robin Hood and King Richard leading to the signing of the

Magna Carta in 1215. At the end of each evening, he bowed and waited with her until her carriage arrived to take her home. A part of her wished that Annabelle was right and that he did fancy her, but she imagined that he was just a gentleman, and that he would do as much for any young woman of his acquaintance.

He in turn observed as Miss Leigh and Mrs. Dove-Lyon experimented and gave his opinion on what hairstyles best suited her, along with which shades of dress would flatter her dark hair and pale skin the most. But the real challenge came when Mr. James tasked her with talking to a man, a stranger.

"Oh, but I couldn't do that," Elizabeth pointed out. "Not when we haven't been introduced. It isn't proper."

He smiled. "I am surprised you don't know ways around that. Many young women employ all sorts of measures to circumvent the rules of society."

"What do you mean?"

"Have you a handkerchief?" he asked.

"Yes."

"Look there. See that gentleman?" He pointed to an older fellow.

"Yes."

"Walk toward him as if you are strolling past him, and drop your handkerchief. He will be honor-bound to pick it up, and from there you may strike up a conversation."

"But it's false. It would be rude."

"Not at all. He would only be being polite in retrieving your handkerchief for you." He nodded at her. "Try it."

Elizabeth hesitantly started forward, and took her handkerchief in her hand, holding it to her eyes. As she passed the older gentleman, she dropped it just as he walked away.

She heard a laugh nearby, and glanced back to see Miss Rowley giggling at her. She felt her cheeks warm, and moved to bend down to retrieve her handkerchief, when a young man knelt before her and picked it up.

"You dropped this," he said, handing it to her.

"Oh, I'm sorry. Thank you," she replied.

"That's funny. I never met a girl who was sorry for dropping a handkerchief before."

They stood there, looking at each other. He was a young man who looked around age twenty-five, with finely combed, brassy blond hair and a square chin. He wore a tightly tied cravat, a tan colored waistcoat and matching trousers, and black boots. He looked rather studious to her eye.

He smiled at her. "I'm new here. This is my first evening."

"And are you enjoying it?"

"Oh yes. So much excitement to be had. What about you, Miss…"

She smiled at him.

"Oh dash it. We've not been introduced. I know, wait here a minute." He walked away.

At that moment Miss Rowley came up to her, fanning herself. She wore a tangerine dress with a square neckline and golden embroidered ribbon around her high waist, with a surly smirk on her face. "My goodness, you do have a way about you, Miss Denham. At this rate you'll empty the room. You're driving the men away like flies."

Elizabeth opened her mouth to respond, then the young man returned with the master of ceremonies. "Miss Denham, this young man wishes to make your acquaintance. May I introduce Mr. Cecil Lewis."

"Delighted to make your acquaintance," he bowed.

Elizabeth curtseyed. Miss Rowley rolled her eyes and walked away, as Mr. Lewis said, "And is this your first time at the Lyon's Den, Miss Denham?"

"No, I've been here before. I've been giving history lessons to Mr. James over there." She turned and nodded toward him.

Mr. James, for his part, looked over casually at them and raised an eyebrow, then leaned against one of the tables.

"And who is Mr. James?"

"An acquaintance of mine."

"Lucky man. I quite like history," he said. "And botany, chemistry, and ancient cultures. I say, are you a student? You're too pretty to be a teacher."

She blushed. "I like to read about history. Plants and chemistry I'm less interested in."

"How wonderful. You are quite unique, you know. Whenever I talk about what I am studying, the ladies around me look bored and lose interest in what I am saying."

"The same thing happens to me when I talk to gentlemen about history."

They smiled at each other.

"I am new to town. Are there any good sights to see?" he asked.

"Oh yes. There's the British Museum, the British Museum Library, the Royal Academy... but you have to apply for tickets for some of these."

"I will have to visit these. I wonder, Miss Denham, if you would care to join me one day?" he asked.

"It would be a pleasure," she agreed.

"Jolly good. I'll see about applying for tickets and speak with you again. I presume I will find you here?"

"Yes, most evenings."

"I thought so." He smiled and bowed, then left.

"Who was that?" Mr. James approached her.

"I've just made a new acquaintance. A Mr. Cecil Lewis."

"He looks rather studious."

"I daresay he is. He knows about history, and he's asked me to join him soon at the British Museum, or the Royal Academy." She felt warm at the thought. A friend. A real friend, who was knowledgeable and whose eyes didn't glaze over in boredom at the thought of past cultures. Who knew such a man existed?

"I do not like him," Mr. James said.

"Why not?"

"A man you've just met, inviting you out socially? It's a bit forward."

"We share a love of history and learning. What is the harm in that?"

"Only that you do not know him."

"Now you are starting to sound like my father. I thought that was the whole point of this exercise, to allow me to meet eligible men. Now you disapprove?"

"Not necessarily. I just think you should get to know him first before stepping out with him."

"And pray, what activities do you suggest we do together in order for that to happen?"

"Dancing. Even if one's partner is a mere gentleman and unknowledgeable about history." His eyes met hers. She opened her mouth to speak, but he bowed and left her.

The next day Elizabeth ran into Mr. James at the Royal Academy. Upon uttering her surprise at seeing him there, he bowed and said, "Good afternoon, Miss Denham. I found that after our discussion last night I fancied a bit of culture. May I walk with you a little?"

"Of course."

They walked side by side and viewed the paintings. There were a number of rooms to walk through and many paintings and sculptures to admire, when Elizabeth stopped.

"What is it?" he asked.

"That man. Mr. Hickson," she said, nodding toward the gentleman some fifteen feet away.

"What about him? Oh yes, the man making the better acquaintance of Miss Rowley. I remember. The thief who thought he could separate a good lady from her garnet."

"He is also shortly to be engaged to an acquaintance of mine, a Miss Plimpett. My mama expects them to announce their engagement any day now."

Mr. James observed the man, who was arm in arm with a young woman who giggled. The girl's dress was a bit plain and worn, and her laugh was loud and raucous. Her hair was mussed as if she'd woken up only recently and hadn't had a maid to pin it properly. When Mr. Hickson's hand moved down to touch her bottom, she didn't slap his hand away, she only giggled more.

Elizabeth said, "I think that is no lady."

"I agree. Perhaps Mr. Hickson isn't engaged after all."

"Maybe not. But my Mama was so certain. Even Miss Plimpett seemed sure of it." She frowned. "Should I tell her?"

"No. Miss Plimpett will not thank you for the information and may even blame you. Have you not heard of the phrase 'Don't kill the messenger'?" he said.

"Yes. But I don't know where it came from."

"Shakespeare. *Antony and Cleopatra*, I believe."

"You are a follower of Shakespeare's plays?" Her eyebrows rose.

He smiled at her. "I have my interests. I like the theater."

"You are a man of mystery, Mr. James. Hidden depths," she teased.

He offered her his arm and she took it, and they spent a happy hour looking at the paintings.

The next few days her schedule was busy, as Mr. Lewis called to take her out for a drive, along with her sister Annabelle, and invited her to dinner the following evening.

That night at the Lyon's Den, whilst she and her mother stood at the gambling tables, Mr. James approached her. "I wonder, Miss Denham, if you might like to join me and attend the theater tomorrow evening. I have a box at the Drury Lane Theater. You would be very welcome to bring your sister or mother as an escort."

Miss Denham said, "Oh, I'm sorry. I would love to, but we are already engaged to dine at Mr. Lewis's."

"It would be very rude to change our plans," Mrs. Denham pointed out.

"Yes, of course. Forget I asked," Mr. James said. He bowed and walked away.

"Mama," Elizabeth said.

"What? It is true. And you have so few suitors, it would be bad form to turn down Mr. Lewis in favor of Mr. James, even if he is the handsomer of the two."

Miss Denham watched him go. A few minutes later she found him in a stairwell and touched his arm. "Mr. James."

He turned around. "Miss Denham?"

"You left so abruptly. I really am sorry, Mr. James. I am due to dine with Mr. Lewis this evening."

"I know. You have already informed me once; you do not need to reject my invitation a second time." His brown eyes were annoyed. He breathed, "I just thought…"

"What?" she asked.

"It is rather soon, isn't it? You've only just met him, and he already asks you to dine with him. Do you not find it a little odd?"

Her eyebrows rose. "You find something improper in his asking me to dinner?"

"No. not at all. Only that he is quick to pay you attention. You know so little of him."

"You think I am being overly friendly?"

"No. I think he is. What is his aim? What are his intentions toward you?" he asked.

She bristled. "I do not know, nor do I care. Is it not enough that a young man wishes to dine with me? We are acquaintances. Is that so wrong?"

"It's fine. I just…" He rubbed the side of his face. "I do not like him. I cannot say why. I think you should not dine with him. Come to the theater with me instead. You and your sister can come, or your mother."

She frowned at him. "Thank you, but I cannot. I have a prior engagement to dine this evening."

"Cancel."

"No."

"Come to the theater with me." He took her hand in his.

"No."

"Miss Denham." His voice was hard.

"Mr. James," she said curtly.

They stood, nose to nose. He frowned at her, and she glared at him. His eyes were like dark pools she could drown in. She hoped *her* eyes were like the stormy gray skies before a storm. She...

He gripped her arms.

"Mr. James, what are you—"

He kissed her.

She slapped him.

CHAPTER FIVE

S HE REELED BACK from him. "Mr. James, what on earth?"

He blushed and stepped back. "I am sorry. My... judgment ran away from me. Do excuse me." He turned on his heel and left.

She stared after him; her mouth hung open. She closed it like a trap and touched her lips, feeling the traces of what had lasted for a split second. His lips had been warm and inviting and had taken her completely by surprise.

They had kissed. How could she look at him now?

She stood alone in the stairwell, wondering what had just happened.

The next evening she stood patiently, listening to her mother's chatter whilst her maid helped choose a dress for their evening dinner. "It was so kind of Mr. Lewis to invite us. Aren't you excited?"

Elizabeth shrugged. "I suppose. But Mama, it is only dinner."

"Yes, but he's inviting us to his home. We will no doubt meet his family and they will like you. Believe me, my dear, this is just the start."

Elizabeth smiled and allowed her mother and maidservant to dress her, fix her hair, and add a necklace to her rose-pink gown. But she could not get Mr. James out of her head.

"Elizabeth, why do you keep touching your lips? Are they dry?"

"No, I'm fine." She put her hand down.

Once they were dressed and stood in the foyer to put on their cloaks, there was a knock at the front door. A footman opened it and received a note, which he handed to Mrs. Denham.

Mrs. Denham opened the letter and pouted. "Oh, pooh." She handed the letter to Elizabeth.

It read:

My dear Miss Denham,

I must cancel our plans this evening. Some food I ate at luncheon turned my stomach and I am unwell.

Yours,
C. Lewis

"Cancel the carriage, Macdonald. We won't be needing it after all," Mrs. Denham said.

Elizabeth frowned as she and her mother removed their cloaks. "We will be joining Mr. Denham and Miss Annabelle for dinner after all," her mother said.

"Very good, madam." The footman left for the kitchens.

Her mother looked at her. "Well, never mind. I hope the young man is all right. What a shame we are to miss dinner. And it's too late to join Mr. James at the theater now, too." She let out a sigh and walked away.

Elizabeth agreed but couldn't shake a funny feeling in her mind. This felt wrong, somehow.

She ate a quiet dinner with her family. Her mother noticed and said, "I know you're in low spirits, Elizabeth. Why don't we visit Mrs. Dove-Lyon?"

"All right." After dinner she and her mother took the family carriage to Cleveland Row, and were admitted via the ladies' entrance. In no time at all they stood by the observation gallery, overlooking the main hall where men and women chatted and laughed together.

Elizabeth accepted a glass of wine from a servant, and drank as she gazed over the crowd of people there, looking for a certain gentleman.

"My word," her mother said. "What do you make of that?"

"What?" Elizabeth asked.

"Why it's Mr. Lewis. Look, down there." She pointed.

Elizabeth followed her gaze and saw that there indeed, stood Mr. Lewis, looking very fit and healthy. Indeed, he rather appeared as so well that one might not have guessed he had been ill at all. He stood near Miss Rowley, and they played hazard at one of the tables.

"It looks as though he is feeling better," Elizabeth said.

"Yes indeed." Her mother, beloved as she was, was also quick to find fault, and Mr. Lewis's health appeared too hale and hearty to be anything else. "Do you think he was ever sick?"

"I do not know." Elizabeth felt warmth in her chest. Perhaps it was the wine, or feeling rejected, slighted, but she felt an impish impulse to confront him and see just what he was playing at. She set down her glass of wine and walked down the spiral staircase to the main floor, feeling heat in her cheeks and a trembling in her hands with every step. She had never confronted a man before. What would she do now?

But in no time at all she approached him. "Why, Mr. Lewis."

He turned around, his eyes wide and eyebrows raised. Fear flitted through his eyes, and then a tight smile lit his face. "Miss Denham." He bowed.

Her curtsey was stilted, awkward and short. Her mother would have laughed to see it. "Mr. Lewis, I am glad to see you looking so well. Are you feeling better?"

Miss Rowley glanced at him and walked off in search of wine.

As they were alone, he said, "Forgive me, Miss Denham, for cancelling our dinner this evening."

"Were you even sick?" The words flew out of her mouth before she could stop them.

He blinked. "Yes. As I said, at luncheon I ate something which did not agree with me and felt it better to cancel our plans than to risk making you ill. You were foremost in my thoughts, Miss Denham, I assure you."

She looked at him. "My mother and I were worried for your health. We were quite surprised to see you here, now."

He had the grace to blush. "Yes. Well as luck would have it, it was only after the dinner hour that I began to feel better, and with nothing in the way of entertainment, I found myself here." He looked at her. "You do not think me wrong, in coming here?" He clapped a hand to his heart. "If I ever thought I had made an error and gave cause to offend you, Miss Denham, I would be mortified."

She smiled slightly. Social etiquette dictated that she behave with kindness and equanimity. What a shame she did not feel either of those things at that moment. "Oh do not trouble yourself, Mr. Lewis. I am not offended. Merely glad to see you are in good health."

"I say, I feel terrible about disappointing you with no dinner. How about tomorrow? We could dine together then."

"I am sorry, but I have plans." She curtseyed, gave him a level look, and walked away.

She did not stay long that evening and confined herself to the upstairs ladies' rooms, where she watched her mother lose three shillings.

The next day she received a call at her home. She put down her book and left her father's library, to enter the family's sitting room, where her mother sat chatting with... "Mr. Lewis," Elizabeth said.

She joined her mother on the sofa, wearing a white day dress and blush pink spencer with puffed sleeves, and sat with her hands folded her in lap. Mr. Lewis wore a gray suit with a paisley waistcoat and a fanciful tied cravat that gave ruffles down the V-neck cut of his jacket.

He looked very charming, made more so by the cheerful look in his eye and the bouquet of flowers he held in his hands.

"Mr. Lewis," Elizabeth said.

"Miss Denham." He bowed. "These are for you."

"Oh?" She accepted the bouquet. "How kind of you."

"Yes well, I thought it only fitting. I felt so guilty seeing you at Mrs. Dove-Lyon's yesterday evening after I'd had to cancel our dinner plans. You made such kind inquiries as to my health, it seemed a bit of blossoms would be a nice gift. I happened to be walking along Carnaby Street and saw these, and thought, *Wouldn't Miss Denham like these?* So here I am." He smiled at her.

"Thank you," Elizabeth said.

"How good of you," Mrs. Denham said, taking them from Elizabeth's hands. "We'll put these in water at once, and then you can gaze at them. They'll look very pretty in your bedroom window, Lizzie." Her mother rose and quit the room, leaving them alone.

"I come with not only flowers, but an invitation. I have applied for tickets and have purchased two to attend the British Museum, tomorrow. I wonder if you might like to join me?"

"I…"

"She would be delighted, sir," Mrs. Denham said, returning to the room. "How very good of you, Mr. Lewis. So thoughtful. But of course, she cannot go unaccompanied."

He blinked. "How thoughtless of me. I shall purchase a third ticket. You must come too, Mrs. Denham. The pieces of history will be remarkable."

"History? Oh no. No, I cannot abide that. Elizabeth tells us more than enough of history. Annabelle will accompany you. She likes to go out, even if it is to see historical sights." She sniffed.

"Very good." Mr. Lewis did not stay long, and promised to meet her at the British Museum at noon the following day.

"We shall be there, Mr. Lewis, you can count on it," Mrs. Denham called, as he took his leave. Once he had gone, she turned to Elizabeth. "Well, what do you think of that, Lizzie, eh? A trip to the British Museum? You'll enjoy that. That is very good of him to do, especially as you both like historical things."

"It is odd, is it not, that he only remembered to buy two tickets."

"Men are often forgetful about such things. Never mind that. Just think, you will have someone to talk about volcanos and Mongols with. And if he likes you well enough, he might make you an offer. Pray, what is his annual income?"

"Mama, it is just a trip to a museum." Elizabeth laughed, and stopped at her mother's serious expression.

"It is never too early to start thinking about these things, Elizabeth."

The following day Elizabeth, Annabelle, and Mr. Lewis passed a pleasant afternoon at the museum, admiring the wild artifacts and marble sculptures transported from other countries, in the name of British expansion.

Elizabeth stood gazing at a Roman bust, when a familiar voice said behind her, "What era is that from, I wonder? The ancient Greeks?"

She turned. "Mr. James." She curtseyed and met his eye, mentally damning the blush in her cheeks.

"Miss Denham." He bowed.

"Lizzie?" Annabelle came to her.

"Annabelle, this is Mr. James. We met that night Mama took me to Mrs. Dove-Lyon's home. Mr. James, this is my sister, Annabelle."

"I remember. We met that day when you lost your dress in the hands of Miss Leigh." Annabelle raised an eyebrow as she gave a pretty curtsey. "Mr. James."

"Miss Annabelle." He bowed.

"Miss Denham?" Mr. Lewis approached and stopped at seeing the girls and Mr. James. "Who is your friend?"

"This is Mr. James. We met similarly to you and I, at Mrs. Dove-

Lyon's home."

The men bowed. Mr. Lewis's face was skeptical, Mr. James's with a slight smile, which did not meet his eye. Instead, he gazed at Elizabeth, who lowered her eyes.

"Would you care to join us, Mr. James?" Annabelle asked.

"A fine idea. I would be delighted. That is if Mr. Lewis does not mind?"

"Not at all," Mr. Lewis uttered. "The more the merrier, I say."

As they walked together through the building, Elizabeth found herself standing beside Mr. James.

"Do you blush, Miss Denham?"

She damned her cheeks. "No, sir."

"It is perhaps the statue, that has caught your eye," he teased.

She looked up, and there was a foreign statue, of a wild horned creature with the face of a man, hooves instead of feet, but most remarkable was the beast's large and extended... extremity. "My goodness."

He laughed. "It is Grecian, perhaps."

"What?"

"The statue. I have heard the Greeks and Romans were very... descriptive in their arts."

"Indeed." She turned and moved along, hearing him chuckle behind her.

"Miss Denham." His voice held a heat that surprised her. "Are we going to talk about it?"

She glanced at him. "What?"

"Our kiss," he said.

She looked away.

He laughed.

"There is nothing to talk about," she said firmly.

"Oh no? I thought perhaps you wished to continue. You seemed to enjoy it."

"You are mistaken."

"You blush, Miss Denham. I think perhaps it is you who are wrong," Mr. James said.

She glared at him, then, and quickly changed her look to a smile as her sister glanced back at them, taking Mr. Lewis's arm, and pointing at a new figurine on display.

"You are wrong," Elizabeth said in a hushed voice. "I have no wish to continue that manner of communication."

He laughed out loud. "Is that what you are calling it?" He looked at her then. "Why do you keep touching your lips, Miss Denham?"

She stiffened. Her hand had found its way to her mouth, again. She firmly dropped it and kept her hands by her sides.

He swiftly pulled her into a small, shadowed alcove. They were hidden from public view, but the wrong look from a single person and they might be discovered.

Her heart beat with anticipation. "What do you think you are doing? Let go—"

He pulled her into a kiss.

She closed her eyes, feeling the soft touch of his lips against hers, reliving that intoxication she had felt just once before and had dreamt about, daydreamed about, and wanted again. Her body moved of its own accord and pressed closer against him, as his right hand trailed down her lower back and curved around her bottom as if it belonged there.

She froze. At any moment they might be found. She gasped, "Mr. James."

He looked at her then, his eyes heavy and low, with long, boyish eyelashes. "Yes, Miss Denham? I simply wished to see for myself whether you truly wished no longer to discuss the matter."

She swallowed. His hands gently pressed her closer to him, and she breathed in, her heart fluttering like a thousand butterflies. She became very conscious of her chest pressed against his. Her voice was breathy. "And what have you determined?"

His mouth curled into a smile. "I have not found my answer yet." He trailed kisses along her neck, making her tense against the tickling sensation. "Not yet." He murmured against her skin.

She laughed and pushed him away. He complied and looked at her. "Miss Denham."

"Mr. James." She took a heady breath, her lips tingling. "I... This is... completely..."

"Right," he said, as she said, "Inappropriate."

He looked down. "I know. I could not help myself."

She looked at him. "I accept your apology."

His gaze flickered back up to her eyes. "I did not say sorry."

"But you meant it."

"No. I am not sorry for it. Not in the least." He released her fully and stepped back. "I will not apologize for doing something we both know is... ill timed, perhaps, but right. I am not sorry for that."

"But you have pulled me into a dark corner. You kissed me," she said accusingly.

"You kissed me back," he pointed out.

She blushed. "I was overcome. You..." Then it dawned on her. "You seek to take advantage of me. Miss Rowley warned me about you. She said you have a habit of ruining young women, then accepting money in return for your silence."

He stared at her as if he had been slapped. "This is what you think of me? That I am a rake? A blackguard? A user of women?"

"What are we doing here, Mr. James?" She asked him, as if making a point.

"I was stealing a kiss from a girl I fancied, and who I thought fancied me back," he snapped. "If I was to take advantage of you, Miss Denham, you would know it."

She emitted a gasp.

His eyes dark, he said, "I had thought better of you, Miss Denham.

I thought you were a woman of principle, who would know better than to believe idle gossip."

"I..." Her hand touched her lips again. "I do not know what to think."

"Oh yes, your precious feminine bluestocking sensibilities. I have shocked you utterly, of course. I should have known." He shot her an angry look. "A word of advice, Miss Denham. Do not trust the word of every young woman you hear, who wishes to gossip. Their words are often wrong, and find their way into the ears of those who have the propensity to hurt others the most."

"Mr. James?" she said in confusion.

"Do not worry, Miss Denham. I will not offend you so again." He bowed and marched away, leaving her in the alcove alone.

A moment later Annabelle came to her. "Here you are. What are you doing here? Where did Mr. James go?"

"He left."

"Are you all right? You look... discomposed. Your cheeks are so pink."

"I... We..."

"Never mind, let's go. I'll say you were close to fainting and need air. It's true enough, there are so many people here it is rather stuffy. Come on." Annabelle took her arm and led her out of the shadows and into the brightly lit display room.

"Ah, Miss Denham. We lost you for a minute there," Mr. Lewis said.

"Sir, I'm afraid my sister is feeling faint. I need to see her home," Annabelle told him.

"Oh, no. Of course. Um..." Mr. Lewis led the way out, through the crowds and from the building.

Once out in the brisk February sunshine, the girls made an apologetic goodbye to Mr. Lewis, who promised to call on them the next day.

As the girls climbed into a hackney carriage, the door shut, and Annabelle let out a noisy sigh. "Oh, what a tiring afternoon."

"Did you not enjoy it?"

"I enjoyed seeing what the ladies were wearing. Your Mr. Lewis dresses well, but not so well as other young men. And he likes you well enough."

"He is not my Mr. Lewis."

"No? Perhaps that is good that he is not. It is a shame you do not like him as much as he does you," Annabelle said.

"What do you mean? I like him."

"Do you? It seemed to me you paid more attention to the Roman busts than to him. Although it seemed to me he is not such a great authority on history as he pretends to be."

"What do you mean?"

"Come now, Lizzie. Even I know that the new world was discovered in 1492 by that Portuguese chap, Columbus. But when you talked of it, he had no idea. He thought the British had settled there, but any schoolchild knows we settled in Jamestown in the 1600s. And that rot he was saying about Henry VIII. He was completely wrong."

Elizabeth smiled. "I tried not to correct him. Imagine his surprise when he learns the man married more than two women."

The girls shared a smile, before Annabelle asked, "What will you do about him? You know Mama wishes you to marry."

Elizabeth glanced out the window. The carriage ride was bumpy and jolted as the horses' hooves clattered against the city streets. "I know."

"But you do not love him."

"I like him," Elizabeth said.

"Do you?"

Elizabeth glanced at her sister. "I have reservations. Mr. Lewis seems so genuine and yet, after he canceled our dinner, he was playing at the gambling tables that very night. He may have overheard I was also invited to go to the theater with Mr. James that evening."

"So? A bit of rivalry between gentlemen never hurt anyone."

"No."

"But why did Mr. James leave so suddenly? It looked like you were talking in that alcove there. I saw him walk out. What is it the novelists say? His face looked like a thundercloud," Annabelle said.

Elizabeth smiled, and her face fell. "We had a disagreement."

"Over what?"

"My sensibilities. And his character."

Annabelle looked at her with interest. "Well, I'm sure he'll come back. He likes you, you know."

Elizabeth blinked. "I'm not so sure. What makes you say that?"

"Uh, let's see. The fact that since he interrupted our little outing, he stuck by your side the entire time, refused to leave, and when he wasn't talking to you, he was staring at you for the rest of it. Mr. Lewis was quite put out. Come off it, Lizzie. Do you have an understanding?"

"With Mr. James? Don't be silly."

"I'm just saying. I know what I saw. Whatever you argued about, I'd bet money it won't keep him away long." Annabelle smiled impishly. "He likes you too much."

Elizabeth threw her reticule at her sister, who laughed aloud.

CHAPTER SIX

T HAT AFTERNOON ELIZABETH received a bouquet of flowers and a note from Mr. Lewis. She smiled at the gift.

Her mother said, "Oh, you will have to thank him at Mrs. Dove-Lyon's tonight. I hear there is to be a great game afoot."

"What game? Is it whist? Faro?"

"No, dear. Something else. But it's only for the young people, so I will accompany you and then be upstairs. Just think, you can play with Mr. Lewis and the others. It will be a pleasure to see you side by side," Mrs. Denham mused happily.

That evening Elizabeth dressed with care. She allowed Peggy to pin her hair back in a less severe style, and wore a lovely rose-colored dress with little cap sleeves, miniature flowers around the bodice, fixed with a light golden sash around the bust to accentuate the empire waist. With a flower in her hair, a light dusting of rouge to her cheeks and a dab to her lips, she was ready.

But once inside Mrs. Dove Lyon's establishment, Elizabeth became less certain. The history lessons had stopped, completely, and she studiously avoided Mr. James's eye as Mrs. Dove-Lyon explained the nature of the evening's game.

"This is a game of chase. Each lady will pick a card, then so will each gentleman. The ladies will go hide, anywhere in this building. Then after five minutes, the gentlemen will go in search of their partner with the same card. Whichever pair makes it back here first wins. Those who aren't playing will get to make their bets here." She stood aside as the dealers stood by to accept bets.

Elizabeth glanced at the other young women. There was Miss Rowley, Miss Dawkins, herself, and the daughter of her mother's friend, Miss Plimpett, who looked very excited, as she beamed at Mr. Hickson.

Elizabeth grew alarmed when she saw that she had drawn the queen of hearts, and Mr. James and Mr. Lewis drew the jack and king of the same suit. That meant they were to find her. Each trio of court cards featured one young lady and two men.

The rules of society were to be forgotten at that moment, for if a young woman was caught by a man of her suit, she was won. If she was discovered by a gentleman of a different suit, they might strike up an acquaintance, but risked losing the game.

"What is the prize?" Mr. Lewis asked.

"A cut of the winnings," Mrs. Dove-Lyon said. "And I will have no interference from the people placing bets. If I find anyone has been tampering with this game or cheating, you will be thrown out."

In no time at all, Elizabeth stood, watching, as the men playing all turned their backs. Mrs. Dove-Lyon said, "Let the game begin. May the best suit win!" and a small gong was rung.

Elizabeth and three other young women went off, running from the room. She dashed up the stairs, pausing at the observation gallery. She could hide under the table of the women's gambling room, but the ladies there might give her away. She could dash behind the musicians, but it was too small a space not to be noticed. She mentally thought of all the rooms she could hide in and instead, her feet took her upstairs, to the third floor.

It was dimly lit, with a series of rooms. She hurried down the corridor and paused before a portrait that looked very old, as if it had come from the time period of the Restoration. It depicted a young man with shoulder-length hair in a severe black suit and tall hat, looking very solemn.

But as she paused to gaze at it, she distantly heard the gong ring again and fled inside the first room beside the portrait. With her back to the door, she hid, breathing quietly.

Minutes passed as her breathing slowed. The handle of the door turned, and she hid behind the door, not making a sound as it opened. "Miss Dawkins?" She heard Mr. Hickson's voice say, then leave.

As the door closed, she let out a sigh of relief. But it was short-lived, as the door opened a minute later, and a man walked in. She didn't make a sound and stood there, quiet as a mouse, as Mr. James glanced behind him and saw her.

He jolted and blinked. Quickly he shut and locked the door. He held a finger to his lips for quiet and paused as the sound of footsteps came near, then disappeared.

He looked at her. "I thought I'd find you here."

"How did you know?"

"The portrait outside. It looked historical. I suspected your curiosity would lead you to this floor and that picture would get your attention. Then it was just a chance of entering the right door." He looked at her. "Besides, did you not think I watched you leave when the gong rang?"

Her mouth opened a little. "That's cheating."

He shrugged. "I play to win. Besides we are both hiding from other people. Miss Rowley has been searching for me and I suspect you are hiding from Mr. Lewis, if I'm not mistaken."

"Very well. You found me, let's go downstairs," she said.

"Wait." He touched her arm.

"What?" She glanced down at his hand.

He ran a hand through his dark hair. "Miss Denham, the other day, at the British Museum…"

"You made your preferences clear. You called me a bluestocking." She turned her head. "No doubt you are like all the others and think me overly educated, unwomanly, and dull to be around. I suspect my history lessons bored you."

His voice was low, and his gaze was sharp. "Stop thinking you know me. You speak such nonsense, Miss Denham, I do not know where it comes from. I do not think you are dull. And I do not find your education to be unattractive."

"You don't?" She looked back at him.

"No." He stepped closer to her, until they stood mere inches apart.

"You talked of my sensibilities as if they were something to be laughed at. A joke. You called me a bluestocking." She poked at his chest, and he caught her hand.

"Let go," she said.

"No."

She looked at him then, seeing his dark eyes look at her madly, as if wanting something so deep and intimate, only she could give it to him. She ached to run her fingers through his dark, tousled hair, feel the press of his skin against hers, and smell the clean scent of him. But she couldn't. The rules of society dictated she must do no such thing, and so she pulled her hand from his and turned her back with regret.

She felt his light touch at her shoulder and allowed him to slowly turn her around. Her breath caught at his touch. She could see him watch the top of her chest rise and fall.

He slowly traced his fingers up from her shoulder, catching her in a shiver, until he stroked her elegant neck. He leaned in, kissed her neck, and she gasped.

He pressed her against the wall and murmured against her skin, his lips pressing each word into her soft neck, and his very touch sent shivers down her spine. By the time he worked his way to her mouth, she could deny herself no longer. She felt positively hungry for him, ladylike behavior be damned.

He tilted her head back and kissed her, his hands working into her dark hair.

She emitted a soft moan, reached for him, and wrapped her hands around his back, pulling him closer to her. Soon she felt her body molded to him, so tight and urgent she felt the need to touch him as she ran her hands up and down his back.

He pulled her close, grabbing her bottom and pressing her tightly against him and up against the wall. He moved her legs apart and didn't mind the fabric and thinness of her gown, as it seemed he wanted beneath her skirts. He kissed her and then she felt his hands explore, having succeeded in pulling her skirts up. Her modesty was no longer hidden; it was on show.

She gasped at the realization, when he breathed, "We should stop."

She met his eyes. He had paused, tensed, his hands on her waist, holding bunches of her skirts. At a word, she might excuse herself and tell him to stop, warn him that he had taken advantage of her, and to never see him again. All might be at an end between them. She did, after all, have another suitor looking for her.

But she wanted the opposite to happen. She didn't want to be anywhere but here, with him, right now. "Yes, we should," she said.

"I do not want to," he murmured in her ear.

"Nor do I."

"Miss Denham, if you do not tell me to stop, I don't think I can." At her curious expression, he swallowed, gazed down at her chest, and said, "I do not think I can control myself around you."

"Then don't."

He gasped.

She took his face in her hands and kissed him, sweetly, tenderly. He leaned into the kiss, enjoying it. But soon the time for tenderness was over, and they both wanted more.

His breathing hard, Mr. James pressed himself against her.

She felt something warm and hard in his breeches touching her, and wondered what it was. This was his manhood, she supposed. Despite being taut and restrained, the friction of him rubbing himself against her felt... delicious. She leaned into the movement, wanting more.

He groaned, moved back and she let out an anguished sigh.

"I will not take you like this. Not here," he said, his voice low. He sounded as if he was trying to convince himself, and lowered his hands from her skirts, letting them drop.

She gave a noise that sounded like a whimper. "Please."

"God help me." He raised her skirts, pulling up her petticoats and making eye contact with her, licked his fingers, and teased her sensitive parts before slipping in between her legs.

Her eyes widened at the touch, feeling him there. Her chest tightened, her nipples hard against her dress. She could see his delight in this and her wide-eyed expression as he touched her, slowly at first, then harder as he kissed her neck, and then tops of her breasts. The slight facial hair on his chin grazed her soft skin, tickling her.

She arched her back, opening her legs, wanting him to touch her faster, harder, more. She felt the slick pressure of his fingers in her womanhood, as he eagerly stroked and petted, probing, and feeling deeper, wetter, heavier as she breathed in time with him. At first, she meekly, then wantonly, submitted to his kisses. She wanted it all. She wanted him, completely. She didn't want it to stop. She wanted nothing more than for time to pause, for them to remain in this room, hidden away, for no one to know about.

She wanted to impale herself upon him, to feel the push and thrust of his fingers inside her even harder, but he kept himself measured and slow, seemingly enjoying himself.

It was agonizing.

It was maddening.

She loved it.

She glared at him, making him laugh as she kissed him, looking into his brown eyes, seeing flecks of almond there. Her breathing was hard, and she knew what they were doing was more than an impropriety, it was positively indecent, but she didn't care. She loved the dangerous look in his eyes, she loved his hand between her legs, and above all, she didn't want it to stop. Her mouth was as dry as if she'd wandered in the desert, and he a source of water that was devilishly good. When he stroked her so much that she came and felt a wave of pleasure rock her body, she cried out.

He slipped his fingers out and held her to him in a close hug. She trembled as a wave of pleasure took her again, making her shudder and shake. He licked his fingers and kissed her mouth, gracing her tongue with the heady sweetness of her own sex.

"My god." She whispered against his chest. "My god."

He gave a little laugh and supported her weight as she slumped against him, just focusing on breathing.

She could feel how wet she was when he eventually stepped back. She felt unsteady on her legs and trembled. "I... How... I cannot speak." Her cheeks were bright pink from the experience.

He laughed. "You look beautiful."

She blushed. "I didn't know that you could..."

He smiled a bashful grin. "It's what I've wanted to do, ever since I laid eyes on you."

"What?"

"It's true. I cannot deny it. I won't. Damn propriety. Damn modesty, and damn all the rules of polite society," he said, cursing with abandon.

She stared at him, her legs still trembling. "Mr. James. I'm sorry, this was indecent. It was my fault; I should never have—"

"No, Miss Denham. I do not want you thinking this was an accident, or a lack of judgment on my part. This was no accident, nor any fault of yours. There was no fault to be had. I won't have you thinking that I do not want you."

She breathed in, and his gaze went to the rise and fall of her chest. "Mr. James…" she started. "This is more than stealing a kiss. You have known me, utterly. I cannot dismiss this."

"Good."

She blinked and lowered her eyes, feeling the blush on her cheeks. "What happens now?"

He looked at her. "I will fix your hair, and rearrange your skirts, and escort you downstairs. I suspect we will have lost."

"Lost?"

"The game, Miss Denham." A smile curled at his lips.

"Oh. Yes, of course. The game."

Once she was made presentable, they slipped out of the room and back downstairs, holding hands. It wasn't until they reached the main gambling hall that she pulled her hand from his, earning a look of annoyance from him.

Mr. Lewis said, "Miss Denham, I found you! Oh." His face fell as he saw her escorted by Mr. James. "Never mind. We didn't win anyway."

They were the second group to re-enter the room, the first being Miss Dawkins, giggling as she was found by Mr. Hickson, much to the dismay of Miss Plimpett. For her trouble, Miss Plimpett approached Mr. Hickson, curtsied and spoke to him, but their interaction was painful to watch, for he simply looked her over and turned his back, returning his attention to Miss Dawkins and leading her away. Miss Plimpett turned red in the face and watched them go.

Elizabeth took a step toward her when Mr. James touched her arm. "Don't. She will not thank you for observing her embarrassment." He looked at her and said, "You blush, Miss Denham. I wonder why."

Elizabeth rolled her eyes and shook her head at him, smiling.

At the sight of Elizabeth and Mr. James, Miss Plimpett scowled and said something to Miss Rowley, who tittered behind her fan. The sight of them conspiring sent a dull thought to Elizabeth's stomach, a sign of trouble yet to come.

"Miss Denham," Mr. James said.

"Yes?"

"I wonder if I might call on you tomorrow."

"Yes, certainly."

"I have a matter of import to speak with you about. That is not suitable for this setting."

"Very well. I will tell Mama to expect you."

"'Til tomorrow then." He kissed her hand. The look he gave her sent a thrill through her, right down to her toes.

The next morning Elizabeth received a note from Miss Plimpett to come at once, as a matter of urgency. Thinking it was something serious, Elizabeth went, and was admitted to the Plimpetts' warm parlor, where Miss Plimpett, Mrs. Plimpett, and Miss Rowley all sat. From the used green china teacups and plate of biscuit crumbs in the center of the small table before the sofa, it was clear they had been socializing for some time.

"Ah, Miss Denham. Do sit down," Mrs. Plimpett said. "I'll leave you girls to talk." She disappeared.

Elizabeth curtseyed and took a seat. "I came as soon as I received your note. Is something the matter?"

"I have heard a disturbing rumor, that I wanted to speak with you about personally, before it reached anyone else," Miss Rowley said.

"Is it true, Miss Denham? Is it? How could you do it?" Miss Plimpett asked, her look harried.

"What are you talking about?" Elizabeth asked.

"Mr. Hickson. We were supposed to be married and instead... I heard it on good authority that last night you spoke with him and told him not to marry me at all, that I was poor. But instead he should marry a Miss Dawkins. Is it true?" Miss Plimpett asked, her eyes wet.

"No. Of course not. I would never do such a thing."

"Really? From what I see, you keep rather coarse company," Miss Rowley said.

"What do you mean by that?" Elizabeth asked.

"I saw you last night, coming down the stairs with Mr. James. Looking very rosy indeed. Have you had a little indiscretion with the man?"

"I beg your pardon?" Elizabeth blushed.

"Aha, you have! I knew it. How could you, Miss Denham? Don't you know he is trouble? I warned you," Miss Rowley said, her eyes brightening like sharpened daggers.

"I don't know what you're talking about. Miss Plimpett, I never spoke with Mr. Hickson. The only time we spoke was here, at your home. I've not said a word to him since." She realized that was not entirely true, considering his attempted theft earlier at the Lyon's Den.

"Of course she would say that," Miss Rowley said. "She's been out to make trouble for you since the beginning."

"I just don't understand. I mean, Mama did always say the Denham girls were jealous of our beauty, but I never imagined it would be true. I thought we were friends, of a sort. Why, Miss Denham? Why?" Miss Plimpett asked, brushing away a tear.

"I never did any such thing. I might ask why Miss Rowley is telling lies," Elizabeth said.

"Hah! It is no lie when it is true. I can see it clear as day, Mr. James has had his way with you. Well, you have no one but yourself to blame, Miss Denham. I tried to warn you. But no, you with your stuck-up ideals and airs, as if you were a grand lady yourself, instead of a girl in trade," Miss Rowley almost spat. "I heard that Mr. Lewis was prepared to make you an offer last night, in the game, but when he saw you come down the stairs with Mr. James, his heart was broken.

He told me later he was so confused. He thought you liked him."

"I do like him. He is a very nice man. I did not know you two were acquainted," Elizabeth said.

Miss Rowley threw a hand in the air as if it was nothing. "Let us focus on your indiscretion, Miss Denham. How could you throw Miss Dawkins into the arms of Mr. Hickson? How could you let your jealousy get the better of you?"

Elizabeth's mouth opened. "I am not jealous." Her voice sounded waspish, even to her.

"Hah," Miss Rowley said. "No doubt you were planning to have your fun with Mr. James and pretend to be virginal in the eyes of Mr. Lewis."

Elizabeth glared at her, at a loss for words.

Miss Rowley glowed with triumph. "Well, I have the truth of it now, so just you wait. The world will know of your little games, Miss Denham. Then no one will have you. What do you say to that?"

"But it's wrong. I never...." Elizabeth's voice trailed off. She had dallied with Mr. James. How could she lie?

"Do not trouble yourself by lying, Miss Denham, it doesn't become you."

"No, it doesn't," Miss Plimpett added, dabbing at her eyes with a handkerchief. "Can we focus on me for a moment? Miss Denham is a liar, but how am I to make a good match now?"

"Simple. Miss Denham here will help you. Otherwise, I will expose her to the world for what she is, a harlot," Miss Rowley said with a smile.

"Miss Rowley." Elizabeth's eyes blazed. "How dare you."

"How could I not, when it is true? I can see the hold Mr. James has on you, Miss Denham, and I pity you for it. Believe me, I know your whole history. How your mother paid Mrs. Dove-Lyon to choose a man to escort you around, and has been paying him to flatter you and pay you attention, to entice other men to take an interest in you. What a shame you actually fell for his charms. Did you really think he was actually interested in you?" She laughed. "Believe me, his attentions are not genuine. They never were."

Elizabeth stood. "Your words are like poison."

"They are the words of a friend," Miss Rowley said.

Elizabeth snorted at that.

"Oh please, do not fight. I have had enough of fighting for one day. What are we going to do about me?" Miss Plimpett asked, flinging her handkerchief to her side. "What am I to do?"

"Miss Denham will help convince your Mr. Hickson to return to you," Miss Rowley said.

"I cannot help it if Mr. Hickson has taken a fancy to other women," Elizabeth said.

"What?" Miss Plimpett asked.

"I saw him, at the Royal Academy. He was in the company of another woman."

"You're lying."

"I wish it were so," Elizabeth said, but her words rang true, and she meant it.

Miss Plimpett shed fresh tears. She held up her handkerchief again and dabbed it against her eyes. "I can't believe you, Miss Denham. We have known each other for years and yet you treat me with such hostility."

"Miss Plimpett, I—"

"Go, Leave me. I don't want to see you anymore."

Elizabeth rose. "I am sorry."

Miss Rowley rose as well. "I will walk you out."

Elizabeth quickly left, at a loss for words. She could not stop Miss Rowley from following her, nor from speaking at her ear. "Admit it, Miss Denham, it is true. He has taken advantage of you and stolen your virtue. If you want to ever have a hope in heaven of marrying anyone, you will listen to what I have to say."

Elizabeth glanced at her. "How did you know?"

Miss Rowley's eyes danced with triumph. "The knowing look in his eye, as if he had conquered a little challenge in a game. The way you acted all meek and coquettish on his arm. It was obvious."

"What do you want from me?"

"He has planned to call on you today, hasn't he? To talk with you about a matter of great import?"

Elizabeth's mouth opened in surprise.

"I thought so. Do not let him in the door, or else you may well find yourself thrown out of your family's house forever. He means to reveal your little indiscretion and extort money from your family, in return for his silence. But if you are not at home, he cannot make demands of you."

Elizabeth let out a sigh. "This is wrong."

"I am looking out for you. What he did was wrong. He should not have treated you so." Miss Rowley blinked. "It is not the first time I have seen it happen."

"What do you mean?"

"It happened to a friend of mine, Miss Lucy Birde. They were courting and from his words and actions, all seemed set to there being a match between them. Her family expected them to announce their engagement any day. Then it happened." Miss Rowley paused.

"Your Mr. James convinced Lucy to run away with him. Once they were alone, he took advantage of her and left her alone in a town far from her home. Meanwhile he returned to her family and demanded money in return for his silence. They refused. She had no money, family, or friends, no one to call on for help. She had no one to rely on. He left her nothing but debts, and she ended up working as a servant to pay the debts before she could return home. By the time her family found her, she was ruined." Miss Rowley wiped away a tear. "She was my best friend. That is why it pains me so to see him ruin another young woman, again."

"What happened to your friend?"

"Lucy? She took sick and died, no thanks to him. If he had done his duty and married her, instead of abandoning her, she might still be alive."

"Good lord."

"That is why I pray that you, Miss Denham, will show sense. Do not let him in your door. Don't make the mistake my friend did."

"What about her family? Did they not sue him?"

"For what? Breach of promise? There was no promise. He'd led her into thinking he was the very best of men, and had her convinced his family would not approve of the match, but if they were married in secret, there would be nothing they could do, and then they could finally be together. Man and wife. It is a compelling dream, is it not?" Miss Rowley asked.

"Why did nothing happen to him?"

"By the time they found her, it was her word against his. They had nothing to show for it but a daughter who had run away and lost her virginity. They wanted to force him to marry her, but he refused. He demanded money, or else he would spread the tale of her lost reputation, and then no man would have her."

"He didn't," Elizabeth breathed.

"He did. A rumor spread, and of course it was true. That she had let herself be deflowered by a scoundrel, due to her own naivety. Her family left town, but not before paying him a fee to keep his mouth shut."

"He blackmailed them?"

"Yes. I only know this because she was my friend. But mention his name and they will tell you. They are warning all good families to stay away from him. No one knows the true nature of their dislike of him, people only think he had affections elsewhere and their daughter fancied him. No one knows the truth, but them, myself, and now you," Miss Rowley said.

"I hardly know what to think," Elizabeth said.

"It is not an easy story to tell. I am only telling you so that you do not make the same mistake as my friend," Miss Rowley said. "Keep your distance from him. Don't give Mr. James the satisfaction of extorting money from your family, when all you did was mistake his attentions for true affection. Instead, you can undo the damage you have caused and help bring Mr. Hickson and Miss Plimpett back together. Help him see the error of his ways."

"I cannot help it if he has a wandering eye."

"No, but you knew about his philandering and did nothing about it. That makes you just as bad. You cannot call yourself a friend to Miss Plimpett having done nothing," Miss Rowley said. "She would not have treated you so poorly as you have treated her, and neither would I."

"Why do you care? We are not friends," Elizabeth pointed out.

"No, but I don't want to see another naive young woman fall victim to Mr. James's charms. You don't deserve that, even if you are a bluestocking." She paused. "I will leave you. Do not forget what I said."

Miss Rowley did not curtsey, and walked away, leaving Elizabeth to return home.

That afternoon, when Mr. James called upon the Denhams at Marlborough Place, Elizabeth was not at home.

CHAPTER SEVEN

E LIZABETH WAS STROLLING in Hyde Park the following afternoon
when she spied a familiar figure. She turned away but it was too
late, Mr. Lewis had seen her.

He soon waved and walked over. "Ah, Miss Denham. What a
coincidence. Here I was just walking along, and I thought of you. Are
you feeling better after the British Museum? I didn't get a chance to
speak with you properly during the night of the game at Mrs. Dove-
Lyon's."

"I am quite well, thank you."

"Did you enjoy the game?" he asked.

"Yes, it was good fun."

"I thought so too. Where were you hiding?"

"Upstairs in one of the old rooms. No one found me," she lied.

"Ah, dash it, I knew I should have looked up there. Up in the servants' quarters, eh?"

"Something like that."

"Very smart, very clever indeed. Well, shall we walk together,
now that we are both here?" he asked.

"All right."

They walked along and talked of history, and she felt a sort of calm come over her as he talked of botany. She thought of Mr. James's hands on her body and what they had done in the heat of a moment. Was she ruined? Had she willingly destroyed her reputation? And if so, for what, a few stolen kisses?

"Miss Denham? You seem distracted. Am I boring you?" Mr. Lewis asked.

"No, not in the least. Please do continue," she said.

He smiled and then said, "Have you heard? There is to be a dance at Mrs. Dove-Lyon's on Saturday. It is to be a masque ball. Isn't that exciting?"

She nodded. "What will you wear?"

"I don't know. I was thinking perhaps a shepherd or a farmer. What about you? We could go as a shepherd and shepherdess." He grinned.

She laughed. "No doubt my mother and sister will already have plans for what I will wear. I couldn't say what I will dress up as."

He looked disappointed. "Well, no matter. I know you will be the prettiest girl there, even if you aren't dressed up as a shepherdess. I claim the first two dances." He faced her. "And I hope you do not mind, Miss Denham, but it is my hope to stay close to you all evening. If that is agreeable to you?"

Her mouth dropped open. "Oh, I..."

He took her gloved hand in his and gave it a warm pat. "You are overcome. 1 understand. And so you should be. It is not every day a young woman has an admirer at her age. What are you? Twenty-seven? Twenty-eight?"

Her eyes widened. "Twenty-two."

"Oh, my mistake. It is your hair, perhaps, that makes you look older. So severe. When I first saw you, I thought you were the prettiest governess I ever saw. If my governess had looked like you, I would have paid more attention in my lessons." He laughed.

Her smile was faint.

The next few days she received a note each day from Mr. James, asking about her health, and if he might call on her. But she hadn't the heart to answer him. What could she say to the man who had ruined her, and she had accepted his attentions willingly? She was worse than a common harlot. She couldn't even lie to herself that it was an accident, for she had told him not to stop. And worse... she wanted to do it again.

The evening of the masquerade ball, she stood dressed in her room, wearing the costume her mother had picked out for her. "A goose? I am a goose?"

"And I am your mother." Mrs. Denham said, looking very fetching in a shepherdess gown, complete with a fluffy white bonnet with many ruffles, and a shepherd's crook.

"You're the prettiest goose I ever saw," Annabelle said, eyeing her sister with a grin.

Elizabeth shot her a look, and Annabelle didn't try to hide her laughter.

"There was nothing else? No other costumes?" Elizabeth asked.

"I know you would have wanted to dress up as Helen of Troy or Joan of Arc, but no one really pays attention to those historical women these days. Besides, this is much more fun." Her mother giggled. "You look darling, Lizzie. Don't ruffle those feathers now."

Elizabeth stared at her costume in her looking glass. She wore a white dress, little more than a day dress, but her white spencer was covered with feathers, from the sleeves to the little cute cap shoulders. The masque her mother tied around her head bore eyeholes and a long beak that covered the upper half of her face, also covered in feathers.

"I would have purchased you a pair of feathery shoes, but they seemed a bit much. No one will be looking at your shoes anyway," her mother said.

"No, instead they'll be looking at my giant beak." Elizabeth stared at herself in the glass.

"If's it any consolation, it's a very pretty beak," Annabelle said.

Elizabeth sneezed when a feather tickled her nose.

"Oh dear," her mother said. "Try not to do that at the ball."

Once inside Mrs. Dove-Lyon's establishment, they handed their cloaks to a servant and made their way down to the main hall, which had been transformed into a large ballroom. Long, thin tapered beeswax candles burned merrily, adding a warm golden light to the room. All the gambling tables had been cleared away and servants circulated with trays of wine and champagne. Women and men danced, some wearing sedate, others outrageous costumes. Elizabeth spotted kings, queens, statues come to life, Greek gods and goddesses, and muses in togas.

"Do you see anyone we know?" her mother asked.

"No, but then everyone is wearing masques," Elizabeth pointed out.

"Don't be cheeky, Lizzie, it's unbecoming," her mother said.

Elizabeth refrained from comment and began to stand on the sidelines when she was soon asked to dance. She was swept up in a quadrille and then a reel, and a mélange, when she tired and begged off, going to the sidelines to gratefully accept a glass of champagne from a servant.

A voice said behind her, "And how are your feathers this evening?" She whirled around. "Sir?"

"Miss Denham?"

"Yes. But you had the advantage, sir, for I do not know you."

"Do you not?" The man wore a dark masque that looked like a red devil's, complete with large grotesque eyebrows and a wide mouth that sneered. He took her hand and led her off to the edge of the room, where there was scant privacy but more air than on the main dance floor. He lifted his mask and winked. "Hello, Miss Denham."

"Mr. James."

He took her gloved hand and kissed it, and said, "I have sent you notes. I wondered if you were unwell. You didn't answer."

"I did not know what to say."

"Why is that?" He did not let go of her hand. "I told you I was going to call on you, but you weren't at home. Why weren't you there?"

"I had business in town."

"Business? What sort?"

She swallowed. "Who is Miss Birde?" she asked.

He dropped her hand.

"Miss Lucy Birde? You are acquainted, are you not?" she asked.

He pulled a ribbon free, releasing his mask from his face. He held it in his hand and glanced at her. "I thought you were better than to listen to salacious gossip. What have you heard?"

"That you ruined the reputation of a young woman, and demanded money from her family to keep it a secret. And when they refused, you spread rumors to ruin her good name, making them leave town." She felt rather ridiculous, for she said this whilst still wearing her feathered beak masque.

"Hah. Is that what they said?" He shook his head. "And pray, who told you this?"

"Miss Rowley."

"Of course she did. And you believed her?" he asked.

"She tried to warn me. To stay away."

"Did she? And that is why you were not at home when I called," he said accusingly.

She looked away.

"So it is true. You do believe her. You think me the worst of men." Mr. James gritted his teeth and dropped his masque to the floor. "Miss Denham, no doubt you think me a monster. But I tell you, it is not true. I will tell you everything if you let me." He took her hands in his.

"I do not know who to believe."

He reached behind her head and pulled the ribbon free, releasing her feathered masque. He took it and let it drop to the floor by her side. "Would an immoral man do this?" He pulled her close and kissed her, hard.

She felt her heart rise again, and with her chest pressed against his, she felt the pounding drumbeat of his heart. It matched the skittish pitter-patter of her own. She closed her eyes and felt his lips, his hands clasp hers, so warm. She felt so hot she might burn.

She pushed him back, tugging her hands away. It had been a good kiss, and she had liked it. But there was too much at stake now. She had already told him her secret, she would not act like a lovesick girl, swooning at the barest touch.

He looked pained to be not touching her. "What need I do for you to believe me?" he asked.

His voice was ragged and the darkness in his eyes had grown. He looked positively wicked. He hadn't wanted the kiss to end either, she realized.

"I don't know." She looked down. "But I know that I am a fool," she said.

"Why is that?"

"Because I have fallen for you," she said simply, picked up her masque, and walked away.

Elizabeth retied her masque on her face and returned to her mother, who said, "Ah, Lizzie. Here is Mr. Lewis."

Elizabeth smiled beneath her masque, and allowed Mr. Lewis to lead her into two dances. Unfortunately, he was not very light of foot, and stepped on her feet more than once. He excused himself to use the necessary when she took the opportunity to sit down.

Not far from her stood Mr. Hickson, who was not wearing a mask. She rose and approached him. "Mr. Hickson," she said.

He turned. "Miss?"

"It's Miss Denham."

"Oh." His eyes glazed over in boredom, then he eyed her dress. "You look like a bird."

"I know. I'm dressed as a goose."

"I see."

She said, "I had hoped to hear of your engagement to Miss Plimpett. Was I mistaken?"

He tugged at his collar. "Not that it's any of your business, but yes, I'm afraid so. We are good friends, but my affections lie elsewhere."

"What a shame. She thinks very highly of you," she said.

He glanced at her. "I had heard she…"

"Miss Plimpett is a very amiable young woman. And I believe she has five thousand a year."

"Know you this for a fact?"

"I couldn't say. But I have known her family for many years and so…" She shrugged. "I have dined at their home in town many times."

"I see." He glanced over at some pretty young women and said, "Excuse me, Miss Denham. I never was one to take advice from a goose. I'll thank you to leave me to my own affairs."

She swallowed and looked down as he left her for better company.

Half an hour passed, and as she stood by her mother, Mr. James returned to her and said, "Miss Denham, might I have a word?"

She looked at him. He wore his masque again but from the stiff set of his shoulders, his formal bearing, and curled hands at his sides, she knew. He was furious. "Mr. James? Is everything all right?"

"No, it is not." He gestured for her to go before him and she did, leading the way to a corner of the room.

Once they were assured of a moment's privacy, despite being in full view of the assembly, she asked, "What is wrong?"

"I have heard something disturbing. You are acquainted with Mr. Lewis, are you not?"

"You know very well I am."

"How well acquainted?" His voice held a note of anger.

"What is this about? We are friends. Tonight we danced together. I love to dance."

"Love is what I speak of, unfortunately," he said.

"What do you mean?"

"I have overheard a conversation between Mr. Lewis and some other men at this party. I must know, has he made you an offer?"

"Of what?"

"Marriage. Has he proposed to you?"

"No. Why?"

"Because, he has bragged to a party of men not ten minutes ago that he expects to bed you, but he will not marry you as he can't be bothered to do more than dally with a girl..." He paused.

"A girl what, Mr. James?" she prompted.

"A girl in trade," he finished and looked away.

Spots of color warmed her cheeks. "I see. And why would he say such a thing? We were dancing together not half an hour ago."

"Did you know that he is well acquainted with Miss Rowley?"

"Is he? They seemed like strangers to me."

"He is her cousin. She has involved him in her schemes to discredit you after you so successfully got her in trouble for stealing, her and her lover, Mr. Hickson."

"What?" Elizabeth stared at him. "I cannot believe this. No, Mr. James, this cannot be true."

"I assure you, Miss Denham, it is. I came to tell you, to warn you to stay away from him. He means you no good."

Elizabeth glanced across the room, where Mr. Lewis caught her eye and waved. She looked back at Mr. James. "He seems perfectly amiable."

"He has taken bets to besmirch your honor."

"You and I both know there is nothing left to take," she muttered.

"Elizabeth..." he started.

"No, Mr. James. Do not call me by my Christian name. It is unseemly, and we are friends, but... I wonder if we are even that. Tell me, did my mother pay you to escort me around?"

He avoided her gaze.

"Did she? Did she pay Mrs. Dove-Lyon to induce you to pay me attention and escort me around, so as to entice other men? All under the guise of teaching me to attract one, in exchange for some history lessons? Was that their business?"

"Miss Denham, please. You are focusing on the wrong thing. Mr. Lewis has wagered to ruin you, to ruin your reputation. Isn't that more important?" he asked.

"I do not believe you, Mr. James," she snapped. "This entire time, Mr. Lewis has been nothing but kindness itself. He has escorted me around of his own free will, not because he was being paid, which is more than I can say for you."

"You don't know what you are talking about."

"I say, did they pay you to kiss me as well? To put your hands on me? How much did you charge them for that? Did I repulse you?" Tears came to her eyes.

"You are speaking nonsense, Miss Denham. Stop it," he told her.

"No. It is you who are talking rot. You are blackening the name of a man who has been only kind to me. Is that your own prejudice coming out, Mr. James? You think that because my family is in trade, no honest man could be prevailed upon to like me for myself? He must, of course, want nothing more than to ruin my good name. Is that it?"

"No," he said curtly. "I am telling you the truth, Miss Denham. He is Miss Rowley's cousin and seeks only to harm you. I am telling you this out of concern for you."

She glared at him, daring him to speak as a tear rolled down her cheek. Hidden by her feathered mask, it rolled down to her lips. "I cannot believe you would talk to me this way. This was supposed to be a pleasant evening."

He ran a hand through his dark tousled hair. "Forgive me for disturbing you, Miss Denham." He bowed and walked stiffly away.

She returned to her mother's side, who said, "Ah, Lizzie. Mr. Lewis is here."

Elizabeth nodded to the young man, who said, "I wonder, Miss Denham, if I might have a word in private? There is something particular I wished to ask you." He smiled.

"Oh yes, of course. Lizzie will be glad to speak with you," Mrs. Denham said.

Elizabeth raised an eyebrow at her mother, and followed Mr. Lewis outside toward the gardens. She followed him, moving swiftly like a white shadow, shedding feathers where she walked.

Outside the building, the ground was lit with small little lanterns, that lit up a path to a small walled garden. In it were trees, benches, a small pond with a fountain, and not ten feet away, stood Mr. Lewis.

"Mr. Lewis," Elizabeth called, taking off her feathered mask. She wiped away the tear from her lip.

He turned around. "Miss Denham, how very well you look. Such a pretty bird you are. And are you enjoying the festivities?"

"Tolerably well, thank you."

He sat down on a stone bench and patted the spot next to him. "You should know, Miss Denham, I think very highly of you. I came here with no other reason but to see you. But you should know, you were the subject of some rude conversation this evening."

"What do you mean?" She sat down and shivered; the stone bench was cold.

"Why, Mr. James was bragging to all who would listen, how he planned to steal your virtue and extort your family for money to keep his silence, so you could make a good marriage. My cousin tells me he makes a practice of it, and that is how he maintains his lifestyle."

"Your cousin? Miss Rowley?"

Annoyance flitted across his face, then it was gone. "Yes. She had it on very good authority that he makes a practice of such lecherous behavior, and when he spoke your name, I wouldn't hear of it. I couldn't bear anyone to speak poorly of you, Miss Denham."

"Thank you, Mr. Lewis. That is extremely kind of you."

"As I said, it is the least I could do. Forgive me, I cannot talk to you whilst you look like a chicken." He edged closer to her on the bench and slowly pulled the ribbon free of her masque, releasing it to the ground. He took her hand. "Miss Denham, I hope you understand, I have strong feelings for you."

She smiled and her heart began to thump. "We are good friends."

He edged closer. "I hope we can be more than that. In my mind, we are very close." He massaged her hand.

She swallowed and pulled her hand back, as he suddenly pitched forward and smacked her head with his. "Ow." She fell back, clapping a hand to her forehead. "What did you do that for?"

"Miss Denham, I am overcome." Mr. Lewis leaned forward and took her in his arms, mashing his lips against hers.

She tensed. This was not the soft romantic touch of a man in love, this was the wet, slithering lips and tongue of a man with no care for whom he was kissing. And his breath smelled. She was repulsed.

She emitted a squeak, which Mr. Lewis took as excitement, and he said, "Oh Miss Denham..." He grabbed at her bodice as she shoved him away.

She scooted too far and fell off the bench, landing on the ground. "Mr. Lewis, what are you doing?"

"I am making my intentions known. Come, Miss Denham." He extended a hand to her.

She allowed him to help her to her feet, but then she twisted away as he tried to kiss her again. "Mr. Lewis, please. Stop this at once."

"What? Why?" He looked at her.

"I like you," she began.

He pulled her to him.

She put a hand against his stomach, holding him back. "But I do not love you. We have known each other for such a short time, it is too early for me to know whether I have serious feelings for you."

He dropped her hands. "Love? You... think I am proposing. Marriage."

"Weren't you... about to?" She became less certain with every word.

He threw back his head and laughed. "Oh Miss Denham, you are too much. You honestly believe that I would...?" He guffawed. "That I'd propose marriage to a girl like you?" He put his hands on his knees, laughing.

Her cheeks heated with embarrassment, and a cold shiver went through her. "A girl like me?" she repeated.

"Yes. I have feelings for you, of course. But I would never propose marriage to a girl I met at Mrs. Dove-Lyon's establishment. Good girls do not visit there to find husbands. It is a gambling den after all." He looked at her. "Oh dear, I can see that is what you had thought. Oh my."

"Then what were you doing?" she asked.

"I was going to ask you to become my mistress, of course. Surely you knew?"

Her blood turned to ice in her veins. "Your mistress?"

"Yes," he said.

Elizabeth stared. "You want to make me your mistress."

"Yes. I thought that with a girl of your charm and my wit, we would be a very handsome pair. Besides, didn't you enjoy the flowers and our outing to the British Museum? Those tickets don't come cheap, you know. I was going to ask you that afternoon, but your mother was so keen that you be escorted, so I had to buy another ticket. All part of the game, I assumed."

Her eyes widened. "I thought you were taking me on an outing.

That you wanted to see me."

"I do. Very much." He eyed her cleavage. "But a man has needs, and I thought you and I were kindred souls."

"Spirits, you mean. I believe the phrase is kindred spirits," she told him.

"Yes, exactly. Just what I said. You're so smart. You're sure to be wonderful company. Won't you consider it? I promise to give you flowers and take you to the opera. I'll buy you pretty dresses, too, if that is what you want. Just be with me," he said warmly.

Her face fell. "You speak with such conviction." She looked at him. "Then it is true. You made a bet you could win me over, didn't you? Deflower me and take my virtue?" Her face turned red, and she was suddenly glad of the dark evening.

He shrugged and gave her an easy smile. "You caught me. It was just a little joke, amongst friends. But don't be offended. Besides if I win, I'll use the money to buy you a new hat." He scratched at his crotch.

She swallowed. "I am sorry, but I cannot accept you. I thought you were spending time with me with a mind toward marriage, not... this."

He snorted. "You do give yourself airs, don't you? What girl in her right mind, in your situation, would honestly think a man of my standing would want to marry her?" He laughed. "You don't see it, do you? Why every other man ignores you? Your age, Miss Denham. You are a spinster. A bluestocking. Any reasonable man would have made you an offer by now."

She leaned back as if she had been struck. "How dare you."

"You are funny, Miss Denham. I like that." He stepped toward her. She backed away.

"Playing hard to get, eh? I'll convince you. Whether through charm or through other ways..." He stepped toward her with an air of menace, and she backed up and tripped over her skirt, falling to the ground. He loomed over her, a leering smile on her face, and she kicked his shin, causing him to scowl in pain. "Witch!" Mr. Lewis cried.

She scrambled backward on her hands and knees, when Mr. James stood between them, shielding her. "Back away, Mr. Lewis. Leave here, before I have you thrown out."

Mr. Lewis glared at him. "I'll have you know, my good fellow, that we were in the middle of a private conversation. Clear off."

"I think the lady has had enough of your conversation. Take yourself off or I will for you."

"I don't like your cheek," Mr. Lewis said, sizing up to him.

"I don't like your face," Mr. James told him.

"You want her for yourself, eh? I should've known. She's a wild one." Mr. Lewis smiled. "Well, I'm not one to take it all for myself. We can share her."

Mr. James took off his left glove and slapped Mr. Lewis across the face with a shock that rang across the courtyard.

Mr. Lewis rocked back from the blow. Holding his cheek, he said, "You challenge me? Who do you think you are?"

"Nobody. But you are no gentleman. I demand satisfaction."

"For what? A girl? She is nothing but a nobody herself. Her family is in trade," he said, as if that explained everything.

"Miss Denham is an honorable young woman and deserves your respect. You act like filth, and show nothing but disdain for your betters."

Mr. Lewis glared at them both. "Fine. Where?"

"Tulse Hill at dawn."

"Fine. But it's not my fault, you know. She led me up the garden path, she did!" Mr. Lewis spat, walking away. "You'll pay for this. You both will. Just wait, Miss Denham. I shall tell everyone just what kind of slut you really are. I tell them you tried to give it away and I wouldn't have you."

"You won't, if you know what's good for you," Mr. James growled.

Mr. Lewis hurried away.

Mr. James shook his head. "Miss Denham. Are you all right?" He turned around.

Elizabeth was gone.

CHAPTER EIGHT

U PON ELIZABETH'S RETURN to the main hall, she was stopped by Miss Hermia, who said, "Miss Denham, are you all right? What happened?"

Elizabeth gazed down. Her feathered masque was in a sorry state, for she'd fallen on it when she'd slipped off the stone bench. Her white dress was stained and dirty, and her white feathered spencer was soiled. "I fell in the garden."

"You cannot return to the main hall in such a state. Are you sure you're all right?"

"Yes, I'm fine. Could you tell my mother I would like to leave?"

"Certainly. If you'll wait here, I will fetch your cloak." Miss Hermia curtseyed and in minutes, she returned with Elizabeth's mother and their cloaks.

"Lizzie, whatever's happened?" her mother asked.

"I'm fine, Mama. I would like to go home," Elizabeth said.

"This way, ladies. If you please," Miss Hermia said, leading them away and down a side passage, which emptied onto the street. "I will call your carriage for you."

Once safely ensconced in the carriage with only her mother to face, Elizabeth's face dissolved into tears, and she told her mother everything. Well, almost. She relayed to her mother about Mr. Lewis's proposition and Mr. James's rescue.

"That dirty bastard," Mrs. Denham cursed. "How dare he? What gives him the right to say such things?" She glared at the window, then at Elizabeth. "You were quite right to refuse him. Why, if I'd been there, I would have given him a piece of my mind." She cursed and scowled and muttered all the way home.

Once inside their townhouse, Elizabeth shed her cloak.

"Lizzie, did he... hurt you?"

"No. I convinced him that would not be a wise idea."

"Good girl. Very well, let's call Peggy to run you a bath, and let's get you out of those dirty clothes. Peggy," her mother called.

Elizabeth retired to her room. She sat in a bath and scrubbed herself till her skin was pink, but she felt discomfited. She had just finished and was dressing when there was a knock on her door and her mother came in, wearing a light house dress and shawl. "Lizzie, I wanted to talk to you," she said.

Elizabeth sat on her bed, wearing a warm nightdress, and tied her long hair up in a towel. "Yes, Mama?"

"I know the events of tonight have been distressing, but I know you are too strong a young woman to let that disturb you for long. You are made of stronger stuff." Her mother smiled, then asked uncertainly, "It's just... are you happy?"

"What do you mean?" Elizabeth asked.

"I know that you had hopes that Mr. Lewis might propose marriage, but I wanted you to know that there's no need to rush. I know I have told you stories of how wonderful it was for me to marry at sixteen, but times are different. I know that at your age, you might not think you will ever find a husband, but I don't want you thinking that just because one man suggested such an option to you, that you have to take it. We don't ever have to return to Mrs. Dove-Lyon if you do not wish to. It was a silly idea, bringing you to a gambling den in order to find a husband."

"And paying for a man to accompany me around," Elizabeth added.

"What?" Mrs. Denning said. "I only paid the entry fee. I don't know what you've heard but I haven't paid anyone to do anything. Well, I mean to say I paid Mrs. Caston, but that's because I lost a shilling to her at the tables. Don't tell your father."

"Mama," Elizabeth said. "You mean you didn't pay Mr. James to escort me around?"

"No, dear." Mrs. Denning's face lit up with a smile. "Any attention that young gentleman has paid you is from his own wish to, not due to any financing from me. I would not... do you the dishonor. You are smart, and have a pretty face. And you have conducted yourself well. You do not need my help to find suitors, I believe."

"Thank you, Mama." Elizabeth's chest warmed with a suffusion of feeling. A bluestocking she might be. Unvirtuous, she might be. But she had the love and affection of her mother, and that was to be cherished. She gave her mother a warm smile.

"You were right to refuse the man's despicable offer, of course, but I wondered about you and Mr. James. It was good of him to defend you like that. You like him, don't you?"

Elizabeth looked away. "I do, but we have a strong difference of opinion that I fear will be difficult to overcome."

"What do you mean?"

Feeling the truth might pain her mother, she shook her head. "I'd rather not say."

"Very well." Her mother rose to leave, then said, "I think you shouldn't be too hard on him, whatever his faults. Whenever I have seen him with you, he has always been attentive and polite. If you recall, Mr. Lewis had a self-satisfied air about him that I did not like."

Elizabeth hid her smile and asked, "Do you know something about

Mr. James, Mama?"

Her mother sat beside her on the edge of the bed and opened her mouth to speak, when another knock came at the door. Peggy walked in and said, "Begging your pardon, ma'am, but there's a Mrs. Dove-Lyon here to see Miss Denham."

"Me?" Elizabeth said.

"Now? At this hour?" her mother said.

Peggy nodded.

"This is rather extraordinary. And she's come to see you when you're just out of the bath. Very well, let's get you dressed," Mrs. Denham said.

In a very quick time, Elizabeth was dressed, and her hair plaited in a loose braid. Due to the late hour, she wore a plain night dress with a warm shawl over her shoulders for modesty and joined her mother downstairs to receive Mrs. Dove-Lyon in the parlor.

At meeting them, Mrs. Dove-Lyon curtseyed. "Mrs. Denham, Miss Denham. I came as soon as I learned of what happened tonight. My dear girl, are you all right?"

Elizabeth glanced at her mother, and said, "Yes, I'm fine."

"Good. I want you to know that I had no idea Mr. Lewis would act so abominably. He has been removed from my house and Miss Rowley with him. She had vouched for his good character.

But I did not look into his background as I ought to have done. I value the safety and security of the men and women in my establishment extremely highly and what happened tonight is simply..."

"Abhorrent," Mrs. Denham said.

"I was going to say sickening, but that will do. I can only say how sorry I am, Miss Denham. I never wanted you to have that sort of experience at my establishment."

"Thank you," Elizabeth said. "I am glad that Mr. James was there."

"You and I both, but then I've known him for years. He has always been a good judge of character and he didn't like Mr. Lewis from the start. I should have trusted him."

"Will you take sherry, Mrs. Dove-Lyon?" Mrs. Denham asked.

"Yes, for a moment. It is late and I won't stay long. But one, perhaps."

"I'll fetch a servant." Mrs. Denham rose and quit the room.

"I wonder about Mr. James," Elizabeth said. "I know so little of him."

"What is it you wish to know?" Mrs. Dove-Lyon asked.

"I hardly know. What is his background? Is it true that he... Takes young ladies' honor and then demands money in return for his silence?"

Mrs. Dove-Lyon raised an eyebrow at that. "Mr. James is a good friend, and if he had done such a thing, we would not have stayed friends for long. He has a sad history, I'm afraid. I know he is rumored to have a scandalous reputation but that is all nonsense, utter tosh. The fact is, some years ago a girl had fallen in love with him, but he didn't love her back. He thought nothing of it, especially when she soon declared her love for another man. This man convinced her to run away with him."

Elizabeth breathed in. "To elope to Gretna Greene?"

"That is what the young lady thought. Unfortunately, the man's plans were not so honorable. He took her to a place in London and had his way with her, then left. She had no money, no connections. She had nothing. It wasn't long before she fell into disreputable company and by the time his family found her, she was in a very bad state."

"What do you mean?"

"The girl was ruined. The man she thought was to be her husband had left her penniless, with debts. To pay the bill at the hotel, she'd had to work as a servant and had soon become easy prey to some of the less honorable men there. She was beside herself, and with child, although who the father was is anyone's guess. You might have heard

Miss Rowley mention it, for it was her friend, Miss Lucy Birde."

Mrs. Dove-Lyon continued, "When Mr. James learned of Miss Birde's situation he was prepared to make her an offer, but her family refused. They blamed him for not protecting her and accepting her in the first place. They made it sound like a breach of promise when no promise had actually taken place."

"They blamed him for their daughter's ruin?" Elizabeth asked.

"Completely. They speak harshly of him to anyone who will listen. And when he did make an offer to another girl, her family refused, citing his past behavior toward Miss Birde's family as abominable. They would not take him at his word, so now he spends most evenings here."

"What became of the girl? The one who loved him?"

"Miss Birde? The poor girl eventually died from a fever and left her family with her child to raise. They were going to give the child away, when Mr. James took it and placed the babe in a good home. But ever since, he has looked for the man who besmirched her honor and ruined her good name."

"How horrible."

"Yes. Mind you don't get into any trouble with young men, Miss Denham. Although from what your mother tells me and from what I have seen with my own eyes, are you in no danger of that." Mrs. Dove-Lyon smiled.

"I consider myself fortunate indeed that Mr. James has agreed to help me find a suitable partner."

Mrs. Dove-Lyon leaned in toward Elizabeth and said quietly, "I do not think he has shown any interest in the young women who frequent this establishment for a very long time, Miss Denham. Can you think of why that might be?"

"No, I cannot."

"Can't you?" Mrs. Dove-Lyon asked with a smile.

"No. Especially when I have heard that he was paid to flatter and give me attention, rather than a simple exchange of history lessons and artful conversation."

"You think your mother paid me and I in turn paid him to flatter you?" Mrs. Dove-Lyon gave an unladylike snort, so quiet it was almost inaudible. "May I ask who told you that?"

"Miss Rowley. She warned me about him the first night I stepped into your establishment."

A smile formed on Mrs. Dove-Lyon's face. "My dear girl. Miss Rowley and Mr. James have a history. I imagine that she saw how honorably he had behaved toward her friend Miss Birde, and sought to have him for herself. She soon made her preference for him known, but after escorting her to a few parties, he found she was spreading rumors about him, and he became rather less interested in her company."

"What rumors?" Elizabeth asked.

"That they were very soon to be engaged. I think the girl was hoping that public sentiment and expectation would drive him into action. But I find that when it comes to marriage, peer pressure rarely works. That girl has been trouble ever since. I'm sorry she's caused you so much grief. She won't be allowed in again. Not she nor her cousin."

"I am relieved to hear it. Thank you."

"So, you are still single. Our plan has not yet found you a marriage partner. What do you plan to do if you are unsuccessful?"

Elizabeth swallowed. "I don't know. I suspect I will have to quit my family's home and become a governess or see if I can join a school for young ladies."

"Let us hope that doesn't happen. I can only say this, that whilst your mother has paid the entry fee for my little parties, neither of us paid Mr. James for his trouble. Not even a sixpence. I daresay whatever interest he has shown in you is genuine, so make the most of it."

Mrs. Dove-Lyon didn't stay long, after accepting a small glass of sherry and making her apologies again. With an open invitation to come to her establishment whenever they pleased, she left.

"Well, what do you make of that, Lizzie?" her mother asked.

Elizabeth felt too tired to answer properly and instead gave her mother a quick hug and went to bed. But as she climbed into her bed and snuggled under the bedcovers, she could not sleep. She couldn't. Not when she knew Mr. James would be fighting in her honor in a matter of hours.

When it was still dark, and the tall grandfather clock in the downstairs hallway struck five, she rose from her bed, dressed quietly, and put on a dark hooded cloak. Wearing stiff walking boots, she crept out of her family's townhouse, timing her steps down the creaking staircase with the sound of her father's snores, and slipped out of the house.

After helping herself to one of the horses in the family's stable, she saddled the animal, a dull gray mare with a sweet temperament, and began riding.

It was still dark as she rode, but she knew the way. She took her horse along a path up through Bristol Hill. She dismounted and walked hurriedly up the hill, which led to Tulse Hill.

As the morning skies began to lighten, she hurried up the steep ground, her black boots biting into her heels. The air was chilly and she tugged her cloak around her tighter whilst leading the horse up by the reins, her breath white in the air.

At the top of the hill, she could make out the tall figure of Mr. James and behind him, a young man in dark gray clothing with a sober expression. This man must be his second, Elizabeth realized, standing beside the doctor who had previously visited the gambling den.

She hurried closer and called out, "Mr. James."

Mr. James turned. "Miss Denham?"

She hurried over to him, her hood falling to reveal dark hair rippling down her back. Her gray eyes were dark with worry. "Mr. James.

You must stop this at once."

He frowned at her. "What are you doing here? This is no place for a woman."

"Stopping you. There is no need for this."

He was dressed in dark clothing and presented a forbidding figure to the eye. Dark boots that shone, navy knee breeches and a white shirt and dark waistcoat beneath a loosely tied cloak with a high collar. He looked down on her and took her hands. "Miss Denham, go away. This is no place for you."

"This is foolish," she said.

"Now you're calling me a fool?" His expression darkened.

"If that's what it takes to stop you from being foolhardy, then yes." She looked up at him and dropped her horse's reins.

He took her hands in his. "Miss Denham, this is a matter of honor."

"Mine."

He looked into her gray eyes. "Yes."

"I don't want you fighting a duel over me," she said.

"You're afraid I'll lose?"

She shook her head and mumbled something.

"What was that?" He leaned closer to her. "Speak up."

She glared at him and blinked hard. "I am not worth fighting over."

He tilted her chin up to look at him. "You are everything worth fighting over. That Mr. Lewis has treated you in such a way as to make you think less of yourself, gives me every reason to fight him."

His eyes held hers and refused to let go. A warm feeling filled her chest, then he turned away. "Russell," he said.

"James," A young man, his second, came forward. "This must be Miss Denham." He touched his hat.

"It's dawn," Mr. James said.

"Yes."

"Where's Mr. Lewis?" Mr. James asked.

Mr. Russell checked a small pocket watch. "He is late."

Elizabeth swallowed and stepped back. At her movement, Mr. James reached for her and gave her gloved hand a squeeze.

They waited. A minute passed, then five, then ten.

"I do not think he is coming," the doctor said with a slight smile.

"Nor do I," Mr. James said disgustedly. "What a..." He glanced at Elizabeth and withheld his curse. "Never mind."

"What happens now?" Elizabeth asked.

"Mr. Lewis forfeits. He has no honor. It is now within our power to abuse his name to everyone we meet, something I will do with pleasure. It is of course illegal to duel, but these things have a way of becoming known," Mr. James said, shaking his head. "But I should have known. The man is a louse, he has no good character to speak of. Of course he would shy away from a duel."

"What will you do now?" Elizabeth asked.

Mr. James bid farewell to Mr. Russell and the doctor, and said, "I'll walk you back to town. Although I could murder a coffee."

At the mention of the word murder, Elizabeth shivered. She took up her horse's reins again and began walking.

Mr. James fell into step beside her. "I never thanked you for rescuing me that night from Mr. Lewis. Thank you."

"You're welcome."

"How did you find me?"

"I knew something wasn't quite right and so decided to keep an eye on you. All I did was follow the feathers. That was an interesting costume you wore that night. Was it a swan?" he asked.

"A goose, I think." They shared a smile. "I was wrong about you, Mr. James," she said.

"Oh?"

"I was too easily persuaded by Miss Rowley that you had an ill character. I knew she was no friend to me, but didn't realize she meant to hurt us both by her malicious gossip." She glanced at him. "I'm sorry."

He smiled. "It is good to see you are your own person, Miss Denham. I knew you had a smart head on your shoulders. It pleases me immensely to know, since I am very soon to be engaged."

She looked away. "Engaged?"

"Yes. Did you not know?" he asked.

"No, I didn't."

Her heart fell to the pit of her stomach. Her hopes and secret dreams scattered like autumn leaves from a handful of words. The wretchedness of it all! All this time, he had been helping her and looking out for her, even willing to fight a duel in her honor. Only for her to find that his affections lay elsewhere this entire time. She truly was a bluestocking, and a fool. "Congratulations," she mumbled.

"I was going to tell you the morning after the little game at the Lyon's Den, but you weren't at home," he said quietly. "Do you still wonder at the lady who has taken my eye?"

"Is she pretty?" she asked.

"Very," he said.

"Smart?"

"Absolutely," he told her.

"Educated?"

"We share a love of history."

She froze. "Is she rich?"

"Yes, but I don't care about that. I love her for herself." He faced her.

"Is she a bluestocking?" she whispered. Her heart beat in her throat.

"Definitely. But she's my bluestocking." He grinned.

"Mr. James." She looked him in the eyes. "Is it me?"

He kissed her, leaving her breathless. "Yes. Marry me?"

"Yes."

The End

About the Author

E. L. Johnson writes historical mysteries. A Boston native, she gave up clam chowder and lobster rolls for tea and scones when she moved across the pond to London, where she studied medieval magic at UCL and medieval remedies at Birkbeck College. Now based in Hertfordshire, she is a member of the Hertford Writers' Circle and the founder of the London Seasonal Book Club.

When not writing, Erin spends her days working as a press officer for a royal charity and her evenings as the lead singer of the gothic progressive metal band, Orpheum. She is also an avid Jane Austen fan and has a growing collection of period drama films.

Connect with her on Twitter at twitter.com/ELJohnson888 or on Instagram at instagram.com/ejgoth.

Made in the USA
Middletown, DE
11 November 2023

42442765R00066